THE WAYWARD HEART

Francesca had loved her unruffled way of life, working in the Lynford bookshop with fatherly Mr. Pinkerton. But it had all come to an abrupt end when the shop was sold over Mr. Pinkerton's head, by his nephew Adam. The news caused the old man's death, and fury overwhelmed Francesca. But when Adam offered her a job in the Paris bookshop, she accepted. Here was a chance to get all she could out of a particularly heartless man . . .

STELLA KENT

THE WAYWARD HEART

Complete and Unabridged

LINFORD
Leicester

First published in Great Britain in 1984

First Linford Edition
published 2010

British Library CIP Data

Kent, Stella, *1930 – 1977.*
   The wayward heart. - -
   (Linford romance library)
   1. Booksellers and bookselling- -Fiction.
   2. Love stories. 3. Large type books.
   I. Title II. Series
   823.9'14–dc22

   ISBN 978–1–44480–414–0

Published by
F. A. Thorpe (Publishing)
Anstey, Leicestershire

Set by Words & Graphics Ltd.
Anstey, Leicestershire
Printed and bound in Great Britain by
T. J. International Ltd., Padstow, Cornwall

This book is printed on acid-free paper

11450077

1

'This isn't the way it should be,' Francesca thought miserably, as she peered through the steamy window of the channel ferry at the rain drilling pock-marks in the grey sea.

For as long as she could remember, all her daydreams had been of Paris. Of elegant boulevards and intimate restaurants, lovers strolling along the quays of the Seine and starving together in artistic garrets in Montmartre. And here she was, actually on her way to Paris, in April, not merely for a brief holiday, but to live and to work.

Not that the weather mattered. That would change. What would not change was the bitterness in her heart, and that was certainly not something that should be carried to Paris, she told herself firmly.

As she mused, the undreamlike vision

of Calais through pouring rain hove into sight and she stood up to lift her two heavy suitcases down from the rack. These held everything she possessed in the world. Not only her clothes, but the few treasures she would not part with, books, photographs, cherished souvenirs.

She slung her grip over her shoulder, picked up the smaller case and struggled slowly down the long queue to disembark. Only a month ago, she too had a home, she reflected sadly, and a job that she loved, and in old Oswald Pinkerton, her employer, a dear friend. And all these things had been swept away in a moment by Adam Preston. And it was Adam Preston who was responsible for her being on her way to Paris.

They were through the disembarkation shed at last and at the boat train. Francesca found herself an empty compartment and, sitting down, rested her cheek against the window, thankful to be alone with her thoughts.

As she watched the comings and goings on the platform, an old man with thick white hair turned to say something to a companion. The twinkle in his eyes and the humorous lift to his mouth suddenly brought Mr. Pinkerton back to Francesca and she swallowed hard at the lump in her throat.

Oswald Pinkerton had taken Francesca on as his assistant in his bookshop in Lynford three years before, soon after the death of her beloved parents in a car crash. He had cleared out a room above the shop to make a home for her, he had taught her about the antiquarian book trade, and soon he had become a friend.

She had been happy there. Perhaps it should have been a dull life for a girl of twenty, but there was security and love, and occasional exciting little discoveries in the work. And there had been Drew.

A smile touched Francesca's mouth at the thought of Drew Falconer, Mr. Pinkerton's grandson. His visits, always unannounced, had been the highlight of their lives. She would be sent scurrying out for special cakes with their coffee, and all work would stop while Drew, who apparently supported himself with some very undemanding freelance journalism, entertained them with stories of his latest escapades.

He was just Francesca's age, but with his curling golden hair and laughing blue eyes, seemed even younger. He had been like some bright will-o'-the-wisp from another world, and now she would probably never see him again.

⋆   ⋆   ⋆

And ironically, Francesca had to concede, as the train rolled majestically out of the station, another highlight of their uneventful lives had been Adam Preston's letters from Paris.

Regularly, once a month, a fat letter would thud on to the doormat and Mr. Pinkerton would pick it up eagerly and read it aloud to Francesca. Adam Preston was Mr. Pinkerton's nephew and he ran one of the most famous bookshops in Paris, At the Sign of the Silver Lute on the Left Bank, close by the Sorbonne. Adam's scholarship was a source of great pride to his uncle, and was apparently almost legendary in the business.

But his letters were not wholly about his work, although there were fascinating stories of tracking down rare volumes in remote corners of Europe. There were vivid cameo portraits of customers — far more exotic than anything they encountered in Lynford — accounts of plays and concerts he had been to, descriptions of the parks and gardens in the spring.

How could a man who wrote such sensitive letters be so callous in his personal relationships? Francesca wondered. She was forcing herself to think of that last letter, the one she had not been invited to share, when the steward appeared at the doorway with his refreshment trolley.

She bought a pack of sandwiches and

a cup of coffee, counting out the unfamiliar francs carefully. Maybe if she ate something it would dispel her feeling of sick emptiness, but any appetite she might have had left her as she remembered the pain of those days.

Mr. Pinkerton had read the letter and the colour had drained from his face. Concerned, Francesca had questioned him, but uncharacteristically, he had thrust her roughly aside and shut himself in his private office. He had not emerged for hours and, when he did, he was never the same again. Long telephone calls to Paris had followed. Francesca could not overhear the conversation, but she could hear the desperate pleading in Oswald Pinkerton's voice. Finally he had told her. Adam Preston had decided to sell the shop over his head.

Francesca had been stunned. It had never occurred to her that Adam owned the Lynford shop. 'But why?' she had demanded in astonishment. But all Mr. Pinkerton would say was that Adam knew best.

'Why?' she asked herself again now. It was true that the shop didn't show much profit, but the outgoings were low. Mr. Pinkerton's only extravagances were his books and his nightly glass of port, and her own salary was modest.

She had asked Drew, who had called to see her one night after his grandfather had left for the small flat that he rented nearby. At any other time the unexpected visit would have delighted her, but that night she had been too wretched and bewildered to care.

'I don't know. I just don't know.' Drew had looked shattered, too, sitting on her settee nursing a cup of coffee. His usually lively face was troubled. 'I never thought Uncle Adam was particularly interested in big profits. Didn't Grandfather give you any hint?'

She had shaken her head miserably. 'He won't talk about it. He only told me that I would have to look for a new job and somewhere to live. Oh, Drew, it's hard for me, but it's a tragedy for him. The shop was his life. I never realised it belonged to Mr. Preston.'

'It belonged to Uncle Adam's father originally,' Drew explained. 'He and Grandfather were brothers-in-law and he took Grandfather in to help him in the business. Adam's father did all the travelling and buying while Grandfather ran the shop. Then, about twenty years ago, he decided to open up in Paris and left this shop entirely in my grandfather's charge. When his father died, Adam inherited both the shops. He'd been brought up in the book trade and he expanded the Paris shop enormously. He's something of an international authority now. I suppose it's a practical move.'

'Well, I think it's utterly heartless!' Francesca had exploded. 'I know this is just a little backwater compared to his Paris operation, but he's dealing with people's lives. This could kill Mr. Pinkerton.'

And her prophecy had come horribly true only two days later when Oswald Pinkerton had collapsed with a heart attack. He had lingered for a few hours, and then, to her horror, he had slipped away.

★ ★ ★

Francesca had looked down at the loved face and a fury, previously quite unknown to her, had entered her heart. She returned to the shop and composed a letter to Adam Preston telling him just what she thought of his action. The letter grew more and more incoherent as she struck out a passage here and added a fiercer one there, and it was a week before she was completely satisfied with her effort.

Then, just as she was about to post it, a letter had come from Adam offering her a job in the Paris shop. The effrontery of it had taken her breath away. Uncle Oswald had often praised her competence . . . her English would be useful with the tourist trade . . . so difficult to even find partially trained staff. Francesca had been very nearly spitting with rage as she read it.

She had torn up her original letter and was composing a scathing refusal to be taken over as a sort of relict, or to assuage his guilt, when she had suddenly thought — why not?

The experience in the famous Paris shop was such that she could never acquire elsewhere. And actually to live and work in Paris would be a dream come true. Why not make use of Adam Preston? And if at the same time she could damage him or his precious business . . .

She had set things in order as best she could at the shop, packed up all her belongings, transferred her small bank balance, bought a one-way ticket and curtly informed Adam Preston of her expected date of arrival.

Over accommodation she had been fortunate. The art master at the local grammar school, a regular customer at the bookshop, who had often regaled them with tales of his student days in Paris, had produced the address of his old lodgings in Montmartre and, in response to her enquiry, his landlady had replied that she would 'be delighted to welcome a friend of Monsieur Dodds.'

And so, almost unbelievably, she was on her way, and getting more petrified with every mile.

What would the monstrous Adam Preston be like? she wondered. She had always visualised him as a rather younger version of Mr. Pinkerton, a slightly absent-minded scholar, cultivated and kindly. But, since his action over the shop, the picture in her imagination had changed so much that he had almost grown fangs.

It was odd that she had never met him. But on the only occasion he had visited Lynford during her time there, she had been on holiday, and, not surprisingly, he had not attended his uncle's funeral.

Francesca suddenly realised she felt sleepy. She had left Lynford early in the morning, and had slept badly for several nights before. Now it was past eight in the evening. The train was warm and very comfortable, and before long, she was asleep.

She woke to find the guard standing over her, demanding her passport. She fumbled in her bag to find it, then, when he had left, went along to the washroom where she freshened up her light make-up and brushed her shining honey-coloured hair.

She looked tired and washed-out, with bluish shadows beneath her brown eyes, but she did not expect to encounter Adam Preston until the following day, by which time she hoped her looks would have recovered sufficiently to give her the self-confidence she needed.

★　★　★

The train drew to a standstill in the Gare du Nord as Francesca returned to the compartment. Dragging her two suitcases from the rack, she regarded them gloomily. It didn't look as though anyone was going to come to her rescue this time. She slung her shoulder bag over her shoulder, and by alternately heaving and pushing, managed to catapult her luggage on to the platform.

She straightened up, pushed a honey-coloured strand of hair off her forehead, and looked around. The station was vast, noisy and crowded. There was no sign of a porter. She hauled her cases out of the mainstream of passengers who were heading towards the exit and took stock of her position.

She had memorised her Michelin métro map, but the journey, involving two changes, was obviously impossible when she was so encumbered. She must somehow get herself to the exit and find a taxi, expensive as that might be.

The crowd had now thinned out a little and Francesca had just girded on her luggage once again, when she saw a man watching her. She did not let her eyes linger on him — she had been lectured on the subject of Frenchmen by several elderly ladies before leaving Lynford — but this man was altogether too striking to pass unnoticed. Over six feet tall, with dark brown hair, an attractively angular face and a long expressive mouth, he leant against a barrier watching her with what looked suspiciously like amusement.

Francesca frowned, drew a deep breath, and had managed to totter a few steps when the man detached himself from his barrier and strolled forward directly into her path. She looked up into dark, almost violet, blue eyes and her heart fluttered nervously. She could manage a put-down in her native tongue as well as the next girl, but at the moment her French had totally deserted her.

Then the man spoke. '*Je m'excuse, Mademoiselle. Etes-vous Francesca Merrill?*'

Relief flooded through Francesca. At least Adam Preston had been thoughtful enough to send someone to meet her.

'Yes, I am.' She put down her cases

and extended a hand, but the man bent suddenly, pulled her to him, and kissed her lightly on both cheeks. Then he released her and Francesca staggered back, surprised and not a little disturbed.

'I'm sorry. You are not used to French ways.' The amusement was back in his eyes. He gestured about him and, looking round, Francesca had to concede that a good deal of kissing and embracing was going on.

She smiled faintly. 'It's not like this in Lynford.'

'I imagine not. Well — you look as though you need a porter. *Porteur!*' He had scarcely raised his voice, but two porters immediately materialised at his elbow. '*Les bagages de Mademoiselle.*'

He set off towards the exit with a long-legged stride and Francesca hurried after him thankful to be relieved of her luggage. Who was he? she wondered. His English was perfect, although there was something slightly French in the rhythm of his voice and in his gestures.

Certainly he didn't resemble anybody she had ever met in the book trade.

Outside the station, the man had made for a large brown Renault. He supervised the loading of her luggage and paid the porter, then settling her in the car, he got in beside her. He turned to her and smiled and she caught a flash of white teeth.

'Have you got accommodation for the night?'

'Yes, I've taken a room in Montmartre. It's just off the Rue Norvins.'

'Then I suggest we check your stuff in and have dinner somewhere, Miss Merrill.'

'Isn't it very late?'

'It's half-past ten.'

'Can we get anything to eat at this hour?'

'Why not? We can eat in the middle of the night if we feel inclined.'

'Well — if my landlady doesn't object to me going out again so late.'

He looked at her in surprise. 'Why on earth should she?'

Francesca fell silent. She was sounding absurdly provincial, but the truth was that she was afraid this devastatingly attractive man could distract her from her steely purpose. You are not here to enjoy yourself, my girl, she told herself firmly.

The car had slowed to a crawl now and the man wound down the window and peered out at the street signs. Francesca looked out, too. She saw narrow cobbled streets of tall blank-faced houses and old street lamps that shone through leafy trees. There seemed to be a multitude of small cafés and bars from which came a sudden burst of singing, or the strum of a guitar. They located the Rue Norvins and drove slowly along it until they came to a tiny square. Together they deciphered the name, Place Pascal.

'That's it!' Francesca cried excitedly.

They counted the numbers until they came to her destination, a narrow four-storeyed house with little iron balconies at every window.

17

'Wait here.' The man got out of the car and rang the bell beside the front door. It was opened immediately and a woman appeared in the hall. Francesca had been expecting an elderly woman, but Madame Bauchet was little more than fifty, smartly dressed and with rather improbable auburn hair. She ran out to the car as Francesca alighted, embracing her warmly and kissing her on both cheeks.

'Mademoiselle Merrill! Did you have a pleasant journey? How is my good friend, Mr. Dodds?'

They followed the still chattering woman into the house. Once inside, to Francesca's intense embarrassment, Madame Bauchet gazed at her in a lengthy critical appraisal.

'*Comme vous êtes belle!* Monsieur Dodds, he always liked the pretty girls.' She glanced archly at Francesca's escort as though to imply that she had lost no time in finding a replacement.

Flustered, Francesca began to explain that she was under a misapprehension, when Madame Bauchet called sharply, '*Yussef!*'

From somewhere at the rear of the house, a slim dark-skinned youth emerged smiling.

'Yussef will bring your luggage up. The room is four flights up. That is not too much for the legs, I hope.'

'No, I shall like being high up.'

'Then we will mount.' She smiled coquettishly. 'If Monsieur will wait . . . '

'Really, there's no need for you to wait,' Francesca said to the man hurriedly. 'You've been very kind, but I am rather tired.'

He turned to Madame Bauchet as though Francesca had not spoken. 'I shall be taking Miss Merrill out for something to eat, if that is in order, Madame?'

'Certainly, Monsieur. Mademoiselle must do as she wishes. I will give her a doorkey.'

The two men went out to fetch the

luggage from the car, and the women started up the stairs.

Just as *I* wish! Francesca thought wryly. Decisions seemed to have been firmly taken out of her hands. This wasn't at all how she had imagined the evening turning out, but, if she was honest, it was considerably more exciting than what she had pictured.

She followed Madame Bauchet up a dimly-lit staircase with a decorative iron bannister. After climbing the final flight, the landlady flung open a door and switched on the light within.

It was a big room with two windows. A bright flowered wallpaper carried right across the ceiling gave a rather dizzying effect, but there was a comfortable-looking bed and chair, an enormous wardrobe, and all the other necessities.

'It's very nice, thank you, Madame,' Francesca said. 'I'm sure I shall be most comfortable.'

Madame Bauchet crossed to the windows.

'*Voici — la vue*. Always the English admire *la vue*.'

Francesca joined her. The room was at the back of the house and from the window, over the ancient rooftops, a panoramic view of Paris was spread out.

She caught her breath. 'It's absolutely beautiful!'

Madame Bauchet laughed. '*Oui*. Always they say, worth to climb all the stairs!'

Madame Bauchet left, to return downstairs with Yussef, who had deposited Francesca's cases. Reluctantly Francesca tore herself away from the window. She made a swift inspection of her room and was pleasantly surprised to find a washbasin, with a well-lit mirror, in what she had taken to be a cupboard. Clearly she was not going to be roughing it too much. She washed her face and hands, and quickly renewed her make-up. A little of the strain had left her face and been replaced by a slightly starry-eyed look that irritated her.

She brushed her shining hair until it bounced on her shoulders, picked up her jacket and bag, and ran down the four flights of stairs.

★ ★ ★

As she arrived in the hall her escort emerged from an open door on the right. He held out a key to her.

'Your doorkey, Mademoiselle. Now the night is ours!'

The lightly spoken words sent an absurd shiver down her spine. She had forgotten, for the moment, how attractive he was. Now, as he smiled down at her in the narrow hall, his presence seemed suddenly overpowering and she brushed past him in her haste to get outside.

'Are you too tired to walk?' he asked. 'The car is a bit tricky in some of these streets.'

'I'd love to walk.'

'What's the room like?'

'Very pleasant.'

'Not disappointed, I hope.'

She looked at him. 'What do you mean?'

'Oh, I thought you might have rather enjoyed *la vie de Bohème*. You could have played the rôle beautifully.'

Francesca laughed. 'Not at all. I like my creature comforts.'

They set off across the square. A single lamp illuminated a chestnut tree heavy with creamy blossom, an old worn bench beneath it, and cobblestones still shining after the rain. It was very quiet, but beneath the quiet there was a faint throb like the heartbeat of a great city.

As they walked through the streets, Francesca felt she could almost catch the authentic atmosphere of old Montmartre as the man by her side talked about the artists, poets and composers who had lived there. Listening to him, her heel suddenly caught in the cobblestones, and she would have stumbled if he had not caught her. He held her for a second and she was disturbingly conscious of his muscular body against hers.

He put her from him abruptly. 'You're tired. We'll find somewhere to eat.'

There was no shortage of choice. Every alternate house in the street seemed to be either a restaurant or a bistro.

'Here, this looks fairly promising,' he said as he pushed open a door in an almost dark façade and ushered Francesca in.

The elderly proprietor, his apron reaching to the floor, threaded his way between the tables towards them and escorted them to a table in the corner. It was a tiny room and, to Francesca's delight, there really were red-checked tablecloths and candles on the tables. There was a mingled smell of delicious food, coffee and French cigarettes, and she suddenly realised she was extremely hungry.

She looked across at her companion and laughed. 'This is absurd, but do you know, I don't know your name!'

He stared at her, bewildered. 'What do you mean?'

'You never introduced yourself at the station. I realise Mr. Preston sent you — '

He threw back his head and laughed, and to Francesca watching him it seemed that the flickering candlelight momentarily gave a sinister cast to his features. He stopped abruptly and leant across the table towards her.

'But, my dear girl, I am Adam Preston.'

2

For a few seconds the room spun round Francesca's head, and the smell that had been so delectable a moment before now merely made her feel sick.

'But — you're too young,' she stammered.

'For what, Miss Merrill?'

'I mean, I had quite a different picture of you. You have such a reputation in your field that I naturally expected you to be older.'

'I grew up among books, among editions and imprints and colophons. Does a farmboy need a lifetime to learn about tractors?'

The proprietor had approached the table and was waiting for their order. Adam ordered for both of them without consulting Francesca. Not that she felt like eating anything now. Events were turning out quite differently from what she had planned, and the only thing to do, however late in the day, was to change gear and make a fresh start.

Watching her, Adam saw a slim girl in a green suit with a cream shirt that set off her creamy skin, deep brown eyes whose thick lashes glinted gold at the tips, and a soft appealing mouth. She looked young and vulnerable and rather tired.

He said harshly, 'I'm sorry, I've disappointed you. You were looking for another kindly old uncle.'

Francesca's head jerked up. She stuck out her chin. 'No, Mr. Preston. Your uncle was quite irreplaceable.'

'You were close?'

'I was very fond of him. When my parents were killed together, he was extremely kind to me.'

At that moment the proprietor arrived with a bottle of Bordeaux. As Adam was filling their glasses he said, 'I was very surprised to get word of my uncle's death. He was in excellent health when I last saw him.'

'That wasn't very recently.'

'It was about nine months ago. I realise that I should have visited him more frequently. Why? Had his health been declining for some time?'

'No, his collapse was very sudden.' Francesca glared at him icily. Was this unspeakable man going to pretend that he didn't know the reason for his uncle's collapse? She said in clipped tones, 'I had, at least, expected to see you at the funeral.'

'I deeply regret not being there. But I was in Prague at the time and I didn't receive the notification until it was too late.'

The proprietor returned with their meal. As he laid their plates before them, Adam said, 'The *patron* recommended the lamb cutlets. I hope that meets with your approval. I generally take their word.'

'It smells delicious.' Despite herself, Francesca began to feel hungry again, and, when she started on the cutlets in their subtle sauce, they melted in her mouth.

For a few minutes they ate in silence. Then Francesca said, out of politeness, 'It was good of you to meet me. How did you recognise me? Is Lynford written all over me?'

He smiled a lopsided grin that did not quite reach his eyes. 'Not at all, although you did look rather helpless. I could understand my uncle taking you under his wing. No, I have a photograph.'

'Of me?' She stared at him in surprise.

'Yes, indeed. Uncle Oswald sent it to me a long time ago. He was very proud of his protegée.' He fumbled in his wallet and produced a small snapshot.

*　*　*

Francesca looked at it. It had been taken quite soon after she had gone to work for Oswald Pinkerton and it showed them together in the little garden behind the shop. It had been a very hot day and she was wearing brief

29

shorts and a halterneck top, and her hair had been scraped back into a childish pony tail. Mr. Pinkerton had his arm around her waist and was beaming at her fondly.

Francesca's mouth curved softly at the memory. 'Oh, yes, I remember it. I had no idea Mr. Pinkerton had sent it to you. Drew took it one Sunday afternoon. He was visiting his grandfather and they dropped in for tea.'

'Did you see a lot of my nephew?'

'No. Just an occasional flying visit. He liked to keep an eye on us.'

Taking the photograph back from her, his eyes dwelt at length on the scanty outfit she had worn. 'I can see that he would,' he said drily. 'And a possible explanation for my uncle's rapid decline in health!'

For a moment Francesca could not believe her ears. She stared at him across the table, her cheeks slowly flooding crimson. Then she found her voice.

'How dare you make such a vile

remark!' she blazed. 'It's highly insulting to me, but that doesn't matter — you don't know me. But if you knew your uncle at all, you must know there could be no truth in such a disgusting suggestion. Difficult as it may be for you to understand, Mr. Pinkerton took me into his life for no reason except pure goodness of heart, and it was for that reason that Drew visited us. Why delude yourself? Your uncle died because you sold the shop. It was his whole life.'

Her voice had risen and several couples at nearby tables emerged from their self-absorption to look at them.

Adam Preston's face had grown cold in the face of her tirade, and she realised that he was a little older than she had first thought.

'Miss Merrill, I had no choice in what I did, believe me. My uncle was getting old. You must have known it would come some day.'

'I didn't. It was a shattering blow. I thought it was his shop — '

There was sudden complete silence.

Then he said silkily, 'Did you indeed? Then I can see that it *would* have come as a shattering blow.'

'What do you mean? What are you implying?' Her usually gentle brown eyes flashed fire at him.

'You are over-sensitive. What should I mean? You were shocked by the sale of the shop and my uncle's death. That is just what I would expect from such a devoted young friend.'

The *patron* had returned to remove their plates and was watching the scene with keen appreciation. Somewhat reluctantly he proffered the menu.

'I don't want anything else. I want to go home — I mean to my room,' Francesca said. She attempted to get to her feet, only to find herself hopelessly wedged behind the small table.

'Sit down. This is not a salubrious district for a young woman on her own.' He considered the menu coolly. '*Le fromage, s'il vous plaît, deux cafés et deux Grand Marniers.*'

The proprietor left to get their orders

and, to Francesca's surprise, Adam took her hand that rested on the table-top in his.

'Truce, Miss Merrill? Believe me, I'm very well aware that my behaviour towards my uncle left much to be desired. As to the suggestion I made about you — I have lived most of my life in France and I look on these matters as a Frenchman. If my uncle's old age was made sweeter by *une petite amie* what is there to criticise? I would say he was to be envied. But, very well — ' his grip on her hand tightened as she struggled, outraged, to withdraw it — 'you assure me there was nothing of that sort in your relationship and I apologise. Now, shall I tell you about your job here, or do you wish to return to Lynford?'

'I have nowhere to go in Lynford — or anywhere else.'

'You have a way of making me feel a brute, Miss Merrill, that I am sure is unfounded.'

'Any time you feel a brute I should

33

certainly trust your instincts!'

'*Touché!*' He withdrew his hand, and some treacherous impulse in her missed its enveloping warmth. The *patron* returned with their coffee and liqueurs, and the cheeseboard for Adam, and he finished his meal in a leisurely fashion, totally ignoring her presence.

Francesca on her part was painfully aware of him. Their table candles had burned low and she watched him surreptitiously in the flickering light that gave an almost diabolical lift to his eyebrows and the wry, sardonic mouth. Once or twice his long legs encountered hers beneath the small table and electric tremors ran up her thighs.

Why does he have to look like this? she thought miserably. Why couldn't he be fat and bald and fifty years old? She began to be aware that the two glasses of wine and the liqueur had gone to her head as the room started to swim dizzily.

★　★　★

'Are you ready to leave, Francesca? You look ready for sleep.'

'I was ready fifteen minutes ago,' she said shortly.

He paid the bill and eased the table out to free her. They stood up and he helped her on with her jacket, his body warm against hers in the enclosed space.

'You don't mind if I call you Francesca? It's the way I've always thought of you.'

'Call me anything you please, Mr. Preston. In fact, I would say you already have!'

She made hastily for the door and was thankful to get outside in the cool night air. Somewhere a silvery bell chimed midnight. They started back up the narrow hill, but there was not the easy contact between them that there had been on the way to the restaurant. They walked stiffly, well apart.

They were crossing the Place Pascal when he cleared his throat and said, 'You've had a long day. Sleep late tomorrow. I'll call for you about eleven to take you to the shop.'

'Please don't bother, I can find my way. I'm sure you have more pressing business.'

'Are you quite sure?'

'Quite. I have the Michelin guide.'

They stood in uncomfortable silence at the front door for a moment. Francesca thought he was going to say something further, but he didn't and she said rapidly, 'Thank you for dinner — and for meeting me.' She found the key in her bag and slipped inside.

Climbing the stairs, feeling desperately tired now, she at last reached her own room and flung herself down on the bed. She had never felt so lonely in her life as she did now in this strange city where her sole contact was her detested adversary.

She was relieved that her feelings about Adam Preston were out in the open. Secret resentment was totally unnatural to her. But that he should bear her some sort of a grudge was completely unexpected. And there was no doubt that he did. He thought her a calculating fortune hunter who had wormed her way into a senile old man's affections for what she could get out of him. And whose behaviour might have hastened his end. A wave of sick anger washed over her at the foul insinuation.

Could she really work for a man who thought about her in such a way? But she had completely burned her boats in Lynford. She would have to tolerate him, at least for a while, and it was possible that she would see little of him once she had settled in.

She got ready for bed, then opening one of the windows, she leant out. There was a soft pearly light in the sky and she could still hear the faint throb of the city.

She remembered how magically the night had begun and tears pricked at her eyes. How could her delightful escort have turned out to be the odious Adam Preston? His letters to his uncle had suggested some sensitivity, she conceded, and once or twice tonight she thought she had penetrated his suavity to some vulnerable core beneath. But basically he was just as she had pictured him in the last month — except physically, of course. And that aspect, she resolved, closing the window firmly on the lure of Paris, she was just going to have to ignore.

★ ★ ★

Francesca woke next morning to sunshine pouring into her bedroom. She looked at her watch. It was just eight o'clock. Sleep late, Adam had said, but how could she on her first morning in Paris?

She jumped out of bed and ran to the window. The view was breathtaking. Half of Paris, from the twin towers of Notre Dame to the dome of Les Invalides, was spread out before her.

She slipped on her dressing-gown and located the bathroom. She bathed then, returning to her room, rummaged through her clothes for something that would give her the self-confidence she felt she needed to encounter Adam Preston again. She finally decided that a cream suit with a black silk shirt, and a black velvet band on her hair, did the most for her.

As she hurried downstairs, Madame Bauchet appeared from the rear of the house.

'Ah, Mademoiselle,' Madame Bauchet greeted her as she ushered Francesca into a large kitchen. 'You have slept well?'

'Very well, thank you, Madame. I feel much more rested this morning.'

'That is good. You go now to start your job?'

'Yes. In the Rue des Anges in the Latin Quarter. It's just off the Boulevard St. Michel.'

'The Boul' Mich'. Lot of rogues there,' announced an elderly man in a thick accent who was seated at the kitchen table.

'This is Monsieur Karnaukhov.' Madame pronounced some impenetrable Russian name. 'He lives on the second floor. He is right. The Boul' Mich' can be *dangereux*. You must be discreet. But, no doubt, Monsieur will take care of you.'

'Monsieur? Oh, Mr. Preston. He is my boss.'

'So?' Madame Bauchet's eyes spoke volumes. '*Comme il est beau!*'

'Yes,' Francesca said shortly. A darned sight too *beau*, she thought. She refused the offer of a cup of coffee and took her leave, eager to explore the world outside.

Francesca crossed the square and turned into the Rue Norvins. She may have risen early, but she had no intention of arriving at work for a while. At the top of the Rue Norvins she found herself in the famous Place du Tertre, the village square of Montmartre. She knew the place was notoriously commercialised in the tourist season, but on this April morning it had an authentic charm. There were a score or more restaurants around the square, their tables spilling out on to the pavements, and a delicious aroma of coffee made Francesca realise she was ready for breakfast. She selected a café and sat down at an outside table, and ordered coffee, croissants, butter and apricot jam.

She sipped her coffee happily, the experiences of the previous night almost forgotten. Everywhere there was an intangible electricity in the air that she could not help feeling part of.

She strolled down to the métro station, bought her *carnet* of tickets and at last emerged at the Place St. Michel.

The Rue des Anges, off the bustling Boulevard St. Michel, was little more than a hundred yards long. The houses, colourwashed in soft faded colours, overhung the street. The groundfloor premises were all shops and the largest was Adam Preston's bookshop At the Sign of the Silver Lute. The sign above the door bore no words, simply a beautifully painted silver lute.

★　★　★

Francesca walked in shyly. Inside the shop it was tranquil after the hurly-burly of the streets. She just had time for a quick impression of endless shelves and galleries of books, before a dapper little man of about sixty approached her.

'*Mademoiselle?*'

'*Je suis Francesca Merrill. Monsieur Preston, il m'attend.*'

His eyes widened appreciatively. 'Ah, Mademoiselle. I was awaiting you. I am Marcel Vachette. I regret Monsieur Preston is not here at this time. Will you permit I show you around?'

Francesca experienced a mixture of relief and disappointment. She smiled. 'That's very kind of you.'

They started on their tour of inspection. The shop carried an enormous stock of books on all subjects with a particular emphasis on art books. New books were housed in the front shop, and secondhand ones were stacked ceiling-high in smaller rooms behind. On the second and third floors were further stockrooms, packing rooms — fifty per cent of the business, she was informed, was by mail — a workroom for minor repairs, a tracing section with a library of catalogues, and a secure room with an up-to-date alarm system for the most valuable works.

She was introduced to members of staff, both male and female, all of whom seemed to have been with the shop for many years, and all of whom, Francesca noticed, spoke fair English.

She wondered again at Adam's motive in offering her a job. He appeared to have a well-established English-speaking staff. A bad conscience would have been the obvious explanation, but his behaviour towards her last night had hardly sustained that.

She was descending a staircase from the third floor when she heard his voice in the shop below, and she admitted to herself that she had been half-listening for it since she arrived. An admittance made no easier by the absurd flutterings among the two female assistants also present. Even Monsieur Vachette seemed affected.

'It is Monsieur Adam! Come, Mademoiselle.'

He hurried her down to the shop where Adam was in conversation with an elderly man. She had forgotten quite how striking a figure he was.

He turned and saw her, and for a fleeting second she thought there was an expression of sensual appreciation in his eyes, but instantly it was masked.

He said formally, 'Good morning, Francesca. You slept well, I hope?'

'Perfectly, thank you.' Her tone was a trifle breathless and she hoped he realised it was the result of her rapid descent of the stairs.

'Has Vachette been showing you around?'

'Yes. I'm impressed. It makes our little Lynford operation seem very insignificant.'

'The Lynford outlet was very worthwhile.'

'Mr. Pinkerton and I liked to think so,' Francesca murmured. Vachette had disappeared and Adam turned his full attention on her. 'Look, Francesca,' he said in a low voice, 'I know we got off on the wrong foot last night, but I hoped we could make a fresh start this morning.'

Under the concentrated gaze of his incredibly blue eyes, she could only mumble stupidly, 'Whatever you say — '

His expression turned insolently mocking. 'A rash offer! What about lunch to begin with?'

'You don't have to take me to lunch — '

'I know I don't. It's my pleasure.' He took her arm and escorted her into the street.

'Why the Rue des Anges?' she enquired in an attempt at civility. 'Is there some connection with a church?'

'Two of the oldest churches in Paris, St. Severin and St. Julien le Pauvre, are close by, but no, the reference is to a choir school that once existed in this street. They merely sang like angels.'

'And the Silver Lute?'

'A lutemaker once lived in the house where the shop is now. Apparently he was renowned far and wide for the silver tone of his instruments.'

'When was that?'

'We know he was there in 1480. This is a fascinating district,' Adam said, warming to his subject. 'The oldest part of Paris. The Romans settled here — their amphitheatre and traces of their baths can still be seen. The Boulevard St. Michel was the Roman road leading direct to Rome.'

★   ★   ★

Glancing at his animated face, Francesca felt a pang of regret that things were as they stood between them. It was hard to remember, at this moment, the Adam Preston whose callousness had caused his uncle's death, and who had made such offensive remarks to her only the previous night. By sidestepping to peep into an ancient courtyard, she managed to release her arm from the firm grasp of which she had become so intensely aware.

Adam continued talking and pointing out interesting buildings and streets as they walked through the Latin Quarter and Francesca listened, fascinated.

'But that's enough history for now!' he said suddenly. 'We'll go up to the Luxembourg Gardens and find somewhere to lunch.'

They left the side streets and joined the jostling throng on the boulevard, Adam once again taking her arm as they pushed their way through the crowds. After a few minutes they reached a restaurant, elegant and expensive-looking, and Adam ushered her inside. Decorated in white and green, it was a quiet oasis from the hubbub outside.

A waiter hurried up and led them to a table in the window where Francesca could still see the fascinating scenario on the boulevard. As she looked out, her lips parted.

Watching her, Adam said softly, 'I wish you would let me show you Paris. There is so much you should see.'

The expression in his eyes made Francesca panic and, because the prospect was so treacherously attractive, she said abruptly, 'I came to Paris to earn my living, not enjoy myself.'

He flushed. 'Do you mean to say it was all work in Lynford? No playtime at all?'

Sparks began to flash dangerously in Francesca's eyes. She said, 'I thought you said something about a fresh start today? No insults, no insinuations.'

'Good God, you are the most touchy creature! I'm genuinely interested in your life there. I'm only sorry I never got over to Lynford while you were there.'

'To check up on me?'

'I admit I was intrigued. Here was my uncle, ticking over perfectly competently, year in, year out, for twenty years, and then suddenly you appear on the scene.'

'Are you saying the work deteriorated?'

'On the contrary. As far as our connection was concerned, the administration appeared to improve.'

Before she could reply, the waiter approached Adam and he broke off to give the menu and wine list his undivided attention. This time their order was decided by mutual discussion, aided by Adam's translation.

When the waiter had left Francesca said, 'I suppose it never occurred to you that your uncle might need more from life than simply 'ticking over competently' like a — an elderly robot?'

'Of course it did. But he was an adult male — in fact he was seventy years old — I left it to him to arrange his own — pleasures.'

'I was talking about friendship, about company,' Francesca snapped.

'I've told you that I regret not being able to see him more often, but I was exceedingly fond of him.' He broke off as the wine waiter approached with their wine. When it had been poured and the man had left, he said, 'You lived at the shop, I believe?'

'Yes, that's right. No one had lived on the premises before, but Mr. Pinkerton cleared out one of the storerooms and furnished it as a bedsitter for me. It was — it was very pleasant.'

'You weren't nervous living there alone?'

'No. Lynford is pretty law-abiding, and I don't think an antiquarian book-shop is very attractive to the average burglar, anyway.'

'But my uncle kept valuable stuff there.'

'Well, comparatively, I suppose. But ordinary thieves wouldn't know what to take, or how to dispose of it. In any case, your uncle often stayed on quite late at night.'

Francesca thought she recognised Adam's look of insulting conjecture again and began to bridle, but, at that moment, the waiter arrived with their hors d'oeuvres, eggs in a fragrant tarragon jelly for her, snails bubbling in a hot sauce for Adam.

★ ★ ★

They ate in silence and then, when the table was being cleared, Adam said, 'Was my uncle still at his old flat?'

'Overlooking the park? Yes. But if he was working late at the shop, I would make him supper and we would have it together. And sometimes he would come in on Sunday and have lunch with me. Occasionally Drew would turn up and join us, as on the day that photograph was taken.'

'Quite a cosy little family,' Adam said drily. 'Did my nephew spend a lot of time at the shop?'

'No. I told you that last night. He lived in London, so it was quite a journey. Roughly once a month, I suppose.'

'More after your arrival?'

'That isn't something I could know, is it?' Francesca said shortly. 'I don't imagine so.'

'You've described what sounds a pleasant routine for an elderly scholar, but for a young woman of — what? Twentytwo?'

'Twenty-four.'

'What did you do for a social life?'

Not a lot, she thought wryly. In this setting her social life would sound dreary in the extreme. But immediately, she regretted the disloyalty to her old life. She had been content — no, she had been happy. There may have been few excitements, but there had been security and affection.

'Oh, dined out. There are some surprisingly good restaurants around Lynford.' She avoided his eyes, remembering the Black Swan's unvarying chicken-in-a-basket and frozen lasagne. 'I like to go to the theatre, and concerts.' To say, truthfully, that one liked to go, was not the same as saying that one actually got the chance very often. 'In summer I went to the coast and swam — or sailed.' She had — once — been invited to make up a crew.

'Well — I would never have imagined Lynford provided such a full social round. May I ask whether you have a boy friend?'

'There were a few irregular escorts.'

His eyes appraised her boldly. 'What an unenterprising lot of young men. Do you ride?'

'I did when I was younger. But I haven't for some time.'

'Perhaps we can ride together. I keep a horse in the Bois de Boulogne. It is very beautiful there.'

Francesca's heart gave a leap of mixed pleasure and trepidation at the prospect, but before she could answer, the waiter arrived with their next course of quail in a sauce of white grapes. Again they concentrated on the delicious food with Adam making conversation about the restaurant and the district in general.

When she had eaten the last delectable morsel and the waiters were clearing again, Adam said, 'I never heard how you first came to meet my uncle.'

'My father was a customer of his. He collected books — in a modest way, of course — we hadn't much money. Even when I was very small I loved to go to

Mr. Pinkerton's shop.

'When my parents were killed in a car crash I was in my second year of teacher training college. It was such a shock — we had been so close, the three of us — that I just went to pieces. I was ill for quite a time. I missed a whole term at college, and when I got back I seemed to have lost all interest. Actually, even before the crash, I'd begun to suspect it wasn't for me. My tutors were very understanding and suggested I took a year off to think things out. I was about halfway through the year when I happened to drift into your uncle's shop. He asked warmly after my father, and I just seemed to blurt the whole thing out.'

*   *   *

Adam was watching her with apparently genuine sympathy. 'I didn't mean to upset you — '

'Oh, heavens, it's three years ago. I should be over it by now. Anyway, your uncle offered me a job in the shop. He said things were getting too much for him, which wasn't really true, but I had been keeping myself with a ghastly temp job, so I jumped at it. Then, after a couple of months, he suggested I moved in above the shop, which was wonderful because my family home had been tied to my father's job and I was living in some miserable digs. It was a very pleasant refuge.'

Adam smiled slyly. 'To say nothing of the mad social whirl! Yes, my uncle had a lot of love to give. His only child, Drew's mother, died young and Drew grew up wherever his father happened to be working. I don't think my uncle saw much of him until fairly recently. About the time you came on the scene, in fact.'

'Nothing to do with me, I assure you,' Francesca said, although it was nice to think that it might have been.

'And what sort of thing did you do at the shop? I recall my uncle saying in a letter that you had taken over the driving.'

'Yes, he wasn't happy about driving any longer — his sight wasn't too good — so I drove him to sales. I did most of the clerical work and correspondence. A lot of our business was by mail.'

'He also said you had developed quite a flair for minor repairs. 'Marvellously dextrous, she handles the books as gently as though they were her babes'.'

'I enjoy the work,' Francesca said curtly, sensing a sneer in Adam's repetition of the old man's extravagant praise.

Their dessert was brought, a sweet-sharp iced strawberry mousse buried in fresh raspberries. Francesca spooned it up with relish and, when they were finished, a waiter brought a big silver pot of coffee, and brandy for Adam.

'I'm afraid you were landed with a lot of responsibility at my uncle's death,' Adam said, as Francesca poured the coffee.

'Mr. Cochran, his lawyer, took care of most of it. He made the funeral arrangements and contacted Drew and other family and friends. He tried to advise you.'

'As I said, I was travelling at the time, and, as my schedule was flexible, I had left no forwarding address. However, I'll get over to Lynford as soon as I can and sort things out. I don't know how much of the stock I shall bring over to Paris, and what a possible buyer might want to take.'

'We made everything as secure as we could. We lodged the most valuable books at the bank and put the best of the remainder in the shop safe. The local police promised to keep an eye on the premises. And Mr. Cochran gave particulars to estate agents and put ads in the trade press. We thought that was what you had intended.'

He had the grace to look abashed at her level gaze. 'There was no hurry at all. I didn't mean to bulldoze my uncle into anything — '

'Then I'm afraid he misunderstood you.'

There was a somewhat cool pause. Adam sipped his brandy. 'Was there anything particularly good in stock when he died? He had an excellent instinct for an investment.'

Francesca narrowly avoided choking on her coffee. Really, he was an unbelievably cold creature. She thought of Oswald Pinkerton's hands lovingly caressing fine old bindings and his reluctance to part with his favourites.

'I don't think Mr. Pinkerton thought of books primarily in terms of investments,' she said in icy tones. 'But there were perhaps thirty or forty books that would fetch a good price — say three or four hundred pounds apiece. They were mostly natural history books with fine plates. They are all at the bank. He was very excited about two atlases he had bought recently. I never saw them because they were kept at the bank.'

'Yes, I know about the atlases, he bought them on my advice. They're very rare and very beautiful, I can't wait

to see them, You're sure they are quite
safe?'

'Perfectly.'

* * *

Adam passed his cup across the table
for more coffee and, at the same time,
the waiter arrived with their bill and to
enquire whether madame and monsieur
had enjoyed their meal.

As he chatted with the man, Francesca
watched him covertly. Despite the de-
spicable flaws in his character, she had
to admit that he had treated her with
courtesy and generosity — their lunch
bill was probably astronomical — while
some of her own remarks had sounded
like childish bad manners.

She managed a warm smile as she
passed over his coffee cup.

'Has my uncle's Will been read yet?'
he asked.

The cup wobbled in mid-air, putting
the snowy tablecloth in jeopardy.

'I've no idea,' she said through

clenched teeth, regretting her moment of weakness.

'I imagine everything will go to Drew. I only hope he wasn't too upset to learn that the shop didn't belong to my uncle.'

The colour rushed to Francesca's cheeks and her eyes blazed in anger. The gorgeous food with which Adam Preston had plied her had not quite blunted her sense of outrage.

'This may be hard for you to understand,' she snapped, 'but Drew was upset only over his grandfather's heart-break and death. As it happens, he was already aware of the position regarding the shop, but, even if he hadn't been, money and possessions are not that important to him.'

'Rubbish,' Adam countered briskly. 'Just because he doesn't dine out at expensive restaurants, or possess a decent suit, doesn't mean that he despises money. He's always on the move for one thing and that costs plenty. Has he found himself a job yet?'

'He's a freelance journalist.'

''Free' being the operative word, if I know Drew. He doesn't seem over-eager to settle down to a steady career.'

'You could take him into your business.'

'Heaven forbid! My nephew wouldn't know a first edition from a comic book and, what's more, he couldn't be bothered to find out.'

'I'm sure he'll settle down soon, Mr. Preston. It's just that he's young and has no responsibilities — '

'For heaven's sake, can't you call me Adam! Drew may be the eternal Peter Pan, but he's only ten years my junior.'

For the first time since she had met him, Adam's composure was ruffled. His black brows drew together in fury, even his fine strong hands trembled slightly. There seemed to be something about the mention of Drew that got under his skin. Could it be that, with his own early heavy responsibilities, he envied the footloose, fancy-free young man? It would have been nice to think it was her own championing of the younger man that angered him, but she had to admit it wasn't at all likely.

She didn't want a second undignified scene like the one in the Montmartre café — for one thing this restaurant was much better lit.

'I'm sorry. It's none of my business,' she said contritely.

'And you'll call me Adam?'

'I'll try to.'

He smiled a slow lazy smile that seemed to cause her heart to turn a somersault. 'Did you enjoy your lunch?'

'It was marvellous, thank you.' She shot him a glance through her thick lashes. 'It helped the third degree along beautifully. So much more civilised than a spotlight!'

Once again she saw that she had penetrated his guard.

'The third degree?'

'Surely you didn't think I was unaware that I was undergoing some sort of inquisition?'

'I'm very sorry you should have thought that. It's simply that I was curious about you. My uncle wrote so much about you in his letters. Even Drew, when he last visited me, talked of you. Isn't it natural that I should be curious about the young woman who had such a strong influence on them?'

He pushed back his chair preparatory to leaving and Francesca did the same, still bemused by his last remark. Every other word he said to her seemed to have some sting in the tail. That 'had such a strong influence on them' — as though she was some sort of Svengali! But the proprietor was holding the door open for them, and the sounds and sights and smells of the boulevard hit them like a blow after the cloistered calm of the restaurant.

Adam took her arm firmly and they threaded their way among the crowds. Conversation was quite impossible until they reached the shop.

At his office door, Adam turned to her with a dismissive smile. 'It may be a little while before I see you again, Francesca. I have to be away on business, but Vachette will look after you. I'm sorry you wouldn't let me show you Paris, but take some time off to explore for yourself. Just check with Marcel first.'

Then he was gone and it was as though he left a space behind him in the air. Francesca stared at the closed door, shaken by the strength of her feeling of deprivation. She had never suspected that any man could affect her so strongly — and in so short a time. She told herself that she knew the reason — the man had obsessed her thoughts so much in the past month that his absence was bound to leave a sensation of emptiness — but the knowledge didn't seem to help. She turned away slowly in search of Marcel Vachette.

* * *

It was to be ten days before she saw Adam again. Without appearing inquisitive, she had tried to pick up clues to his movements from Marcel Vachette and it seemed that he had gone to Lynford to oversee the rounding up of the business, then on to London for a few days, finishing up with a weekend on the Riviera.

In the meantime, her own time was full and interesting, if occasionally a little lonely. She settled into the routine of the Silver Lute and was relieved to find no resentment from any of the long-term staff, but only friendliness and patience.

Only four of the staff were full-time. Vachette; Nicole, fortyish and unmarried, dark, thin and quick; Celestine, in total contrast, a big motherly Burgundian; and Henri, very old and silent. All had worked for the Prestons, father and son, for many years. Extra student labour was taken on from the Sorbonne, and the many other schools in the neighbourhood, for busy periods and in the summer season.

Although Francesca was still able to see no reason for Adam hiring her, she soon found a niche and was able to make herself useful. The unusually fine spring had brought early crowds to the capital and the shop was very busy. Marcel Vachette and Nicole did most of the serving, but quite often Francesca found herself called on to help out, particularly in dealing with English-speaking customers.

Without taking the time off work that Adam had offered, she started to explore Paris. She spent her first Sunday at the Louvre, and on her half-day and in the early evenings, she visited some of the justifiably famous sights — the cathedral of Notre Dame, the Arc de Triomphe, the Champs Elysées and the Eiffel Tower.

It was in the evenings that the loneliness hit her, after she hurried home from a café meal — women did not sit alone after dark in Montmartre — or finished a cold meal in her room. It was not extreme, just a sort of vague melancholy that made her wonder whether the famous *l'heure bleu* referred to this sadness of the spirit as much as the bluish light that seemed to hang over the city at dusk.

No one in Paris ever seemed to be alone. In the cafés and bars groups of friends laughed and argued, on the boulevards pairs of lovers and sedate families strolled together.

She would sit at her window and look out over the city with its golden lights, the muted hum of traffic rising to her, and think of the meetings and partings of all the friends and lovers.

The day Adam returned to Paris, Francesca was in the workroom with Celestine and Nicole, packing books for the mail. Celestine was relating tales of her youth in a mixture of English and French, punctuated by gales of laughter. Nicole, a born Parisian, was warning Francesca against picking up Celestine's 'orrible accent', when suddenly she crossed to the door, opened it quietly, listened for a moment, then turned back to the room and announced, 'Monsieur Adam is back, and he has Madame with him.'

3

Francesca would not have thought it possible that her heart could lurch so sickeningly, and, for the first time, she admitted to herself that in the past ten days, deep inside her, there had been a longing to see him again.

But *Madame?* Never for a moment had it occurred to her that Adam Preston was married. On the contrary, she would have said he had all the arrogant independence of the born bachelor.

Now she, too, could smell the faint expensive perfume that had alerted Nicole. She looked down in dismay at the enveloping black cotton smock that Henri had lent her as protection against the workroom dust. She contemplated dragging it over her head, but settled for smoothing back her hair with sticky fingers as she heard Adam's quick, light footsteps on the staircase outside.

The door burst open and he was there, slightly tanned from his Riviera trip, wearing a beautifully-cut formal suit and a dark tie and looking even more devastatingly attractive than Francesca remembered. He looked down at her, taking in the voluminous smock covering her to the calf and the ink smudge across her nose, and a slow smile lifted the corners of his mobile mouth.

'Ah, *la vie de Bohème* has got to you, Francesca. Let me guess — it's Toulouse Lautrec?'

Her heart thudded in her throat so that she could scarcely speak and she felt the colour rush to her cheeks. 'Henri lent me his smock,' she stammered. 'It's dusty in here. I was wearing a light dress.'

'But it's very fetching.' He greeted Celestine and Nicole, talking to the latter about shop business for a few minutes before turning to leave.

'I'm taking Madame to lunch. I'll be back aound three o'clock. I'd like to speak to you then, Francesca.'

He was gone as suddenly as he had arrived.

'Come, come, *vite!*' Nicole was pulling at her wrist. 'Come to the front window and see what Madame is wearing. Now you will see the true Parisian *chic!*'

Reluctantly Francesca allowed herself to be dragged across the landing to the window overlooking the street. Alongside the eager Nicole, she looked down. Adam and his companion were crossing the road, heads together and talking intimately. As she watched his head went back as he laughed at some remark from the woman.

'If he looks up, I'll die!' Francesca thought. She tore her eyes from Adam and concentrated on his companion and her heart sank. The *chic*, as Nicole had promised, was formidable, but the woman would have turned heads in the cheapest chainstore garment. Tall and slender, with perfect features and glossy, beautifully coiffured, black hair, her clothes were simple, but supremely elegant. A toffee-coloured suede suit, as pliable as silk, a designer scarf knotted at the throat, and toning bag, gloves and pumps in the finest kid.

'Is she not elegant?' Nicole breathed in her ear.

'Yes, she is. She's very beautiful,' Francesca said hollowly. She stepped back into the shadow of the landing. 'I had no idea Mr. Preston was married.'

'Oh, he is not,' Nicole laughed. 'No marriage for that one! That is his friend, Madame de Montbel.'

Francesca's heart started on an upward swing that was arrested halfway. 'Friend' was a word that could have a different connotation in France and certainly Adam and Madame de Montbel had looked as intimate as any lovers.

She waited, but Nicole volunteered no further information. Celestine, who had joined them, said, 'Madame is the wife of Gaston de Montbel, an *aristo* from a very old family.' She added, in case Francesca wasn't sufficiently impressed,

'He has great wealth.'

'It looks as though he would need it,' Francesca muttered sourly, as the three of them straggled back to work.

*   *   *

She would have liked to recapture the enjoyable camaraderie of the morning, but, although Nicole and Celestine chattered on, her own feelings were in turmoil. She was appalled at the effect Adam was capable of producing in her. Why on earth should it matter to her that he was romantically involved with another man's wife? In fact, it was just the sort of behaviour she would have expected from him. She despised herself for being so easily swayed from her purpose. She had come to Paris hoping in some way to avenge her old friend, or, at least, to show Adam Preston just what she thought of him, and here she was, going weak at the knees like a silly schoolgirl at his merest glance.

She glanced at the clock and saw it was twenty-to-three. Adam's statement that he wanted to see her on his return had been pushed to the back of her mind, but now it was suddenly dominant. What could he wish to say to her? His tone had been rather stern. Had there been something amiss at Lynford? Something for which she was responsible?

Her mouth went dry at the thought of the coming interview. She slipped out of the room and along to the tiny cloakroom. Her face, looking back at her from the mirror, was pale and wide-eyed, and discovering the black smudge across her nose did nothing for her confidence. She pulled off Henri's smock, combed through her hair and touched up her make-up. Then giving herself a rather shaky smile in the mirror, she smoothed the pale-blue cotton dress down over her hips, and stepped out on to the landing.

To her dismay, Adam was just entering the shop below her and

Madame de Montbel was with him. As she stood rooted to the spot, he looked up and saw her.

'Oh, there you are, Francesca! Gabrielle tells me I am very remiss not to have introduced you. She insisted on coming back with me to meet you.'

He waited as, with leaden feet, Francesca descended the staircase. As she came, the Frenchwoman's eyes were on her, scrutinising her minutely.

Francesca regarded her in return. Close up, she was no less beautiful, but somewhat older, probably around thirty-five, and a good deal of artifice had gone into her looks.

She smiled down at Francesca, warmly enough, if a trifle condescendingly.

'But she is charming, Adam!' she exclaimed. 'Now I understand why you hide her away!' Her English was excellent, with just a slight, attractive accent. 'He talks so much about you, my dear,' she confided to Francesca, 'but never once does he say how pretty you are.'

Francesca avoided looking at Adam. 'I think Mr. Preston is more interested in other attributes of mine,' she replied.

'Not at all,' said Adam. 'But I seem to be out of favour when I credit you with feminine allurement.'

'No. Only the use I supposedly make of my allurement.'

A slight frown of irritation appeared between Gabrielle's perfect eyebrows at being excluded from their conversation.

'Have you seen much of Paris?' she asked Francesca.

'I've made a start. I've been to the Louvre and Notre Dame and Les Invalides and the Arc de Triomphe — '

'And the Eiffel Tower? *Tiens!*' Gabrielle grimaced. 'Nothing but the monuments! What do you do for fun?'

'I enjoyed it,' Francesca said defensively. 'I haven't been out at night very much, because — ' she faltered.

'You have no companion?' Gabrielle said shrewdly. 'We must do something about that. Adam, *chéri*, surely you know some nice young men?'

'Not as many as you, Gabrielle. In any case, I suspect Francesca's heart is already engaged.'

'Then he must come to Paris for a little holiday. Does he work? Can he get away?'

'I was referring to Drew, so I don't suppose that would be any problem,' Adam responded.

Gabrielle's face lit up. 'Ah, you know Drew? He is *adorable*, is he not? I too would enjoy that he came to Paris.'

Witnessing the scowl on Adam's face, Francesca understood, all too clearly, his animosity to Drew. And she had thought it might have something to do with her! How idiotically conceited could one get?

She began a stumbling denial of any relationship with Drew, but Gabrielle had lost interest. 'I must fly — I am due at Balmain at four. Adam, I order you, you must bring Francesca to dine. Let me see — on Sunday, seven-thirty. Don't forget, *chéri!*' She kissed Adam on the cheek, flashed a dazzling smile at

Francesca, and flitted from the shop like some brilliant butterfly.

* * *

Left alone with Francesca, Adam had the grace to look uncomfortable. 'I'm sorry I said what I did about you and Drew. I don't know why I did — '

'It must be because you're such a romantic! Always seeing romance where none exists — ' The brave attempt at a quip died on her lips in the face of his still-thunderous expression. 'I admit I like Drew,' she said. 'I enjoy his company.'

'Well — be that as it may — I shouldn't have said it in front of a third person. It was crass. Can you spare me a minute now?'

'Of course.' She preceded him up the stairs and into his office. He motioned her to an old velvet armchair and sat down behind his desk. A shaft of sunlight, freckled with dust, lit the dark room, and its harsh brightness showed up a hint of strain in his face.

'So,' he began. 'How has it really been? Have you been enjoying yourself? I hope you haven't been too lonely?'

'I haven't been lonely at all, and I enjoy working here very much. I've been discovering the neighbourhood.'

'I thought I wouldn't need to worry about you. Gabrielle simply couldn't conceive of spending time alone, but I knew you would have inner resources.'

Once again, Francesca didn't know how to take his words. Even in what appeared to be a compliment, there seemed a suggestion of criticism.

She said, 'I suppose I'm used to my own company.'

'Well, I'm sure it's a matter of choice. It would surprise me if you had any difficulty finding willing escorts. But I wanted to talk to you about affairs back in Lynford.'

'I hope everything was in order,' Francesca said apprehensively.

'Very much so. You did an excellent job in the short time you had

— considering the sadness — ' his voice faltered, but in a moment he had recovered. 'I've had about half the stock crated up to be brought over here, together with all my uncle's records. I've seen Cochran and he seems to have everything under control. Incidentally, I notice you were paid an extremely small salary. Didn't you have difficulty managing?'

'Well — I had my room.'

'All the same, I would have thought you could have done much better for yourself.'

'I wasn't particularly interested in doing better for myself. I told you why I took the job. Perhaps your uncle didn't think he should take any more out of your profits.'

The childish jibe struck home and a dull flush rose to his cheeks. 'I think he knew me better than that,' he ground between clenched teeth. He went on to ask her what she had been doing at the Silver Lute and she detailed the work she had undertaken, praising the

79

kindness and helpfulness of the staff.

'Good,' said Adam. 'Now the other thing I wanted to tell you was that I saw Drew when I was in London and it seems he's coming over to visit us soon.'

He was watching her closely for some reaction to his words, and some imp of mischief made her exaggerate her pleasure. 'That's wonderful!' she cried gaily. 'Did he say when?'

Her response had an effect. His long, mobile mouth hardened. 'No, he didn't. I'm afraid you'll just have to curb your impatience.' There was a pause and then he said, 'Does he have a girl friend?'

Francesca stared at him, surprised. 'Drew? I've no idea. He never brought anyone to Lynford.'

'He never mentioned one?'

'No.' She had no difficulty in answering. For Drew to have spoken of a girl would have been highly upsetting — at least, Francesca was forced to admit, until she had met his uncle.

'I just wondered. Sometimes I feel I haven't taken the interest in him that I should have done.'

He didn't meet her eyes and for the first time, she sensed a lack of candour in him.

He was silent for a while, and Francesca rose from her chair uncertainly. 'If that's all?'

He looked up. 'Oh, yes. Thank you, Francesca.'

She went to the door, but, when she reached it, she hesitated and turned back to him.

'About your friend — Madame de Montbel's — invitation. I'm aware that she rather wished it on you. I just wanted to say that — that you don't have to go through with it. You could say I wasn't well, or had a previous engagement — '

He looked at her standing in the doorway, tense with embarrassment. A slim figure in a simple pale blue dress, a faint flush warming her creamy skin.

'I'm afraid that wouldn't work,' he said. 'Gabrielle is very persistent when she gets a bee in her bonnet. She'd only come up with another date.' He smiled at her and she felt her knees go weak. 'It looks as though we're stuck with each other!'

* * *

Francesca returned slowly to the workroom. She felt a sheer blind panic at the thought of Gabrielle's dinner party. Nicole had overheard the invitation, and she and Celestine were waiting for Francesca in a state of high excitement that soon crystallised into one question. What was Francesca going to wear?

What indeed? The problem that had been hovering at the edge of her mind like a small black cloud now hit her with the force of a punch in the stomach. It was obvious from Nicole and Celestine's faces that nothing they had seen of her wardrobe, so far, would meet the occasion.

'Madame is very *chic* — very smart,'

Nicole kept repeating until Francesca could have shaken her. 'Of course, she will not expect too much of you — being English — but you will not want to let Monsieur Adam down.'

Francesca thought for a moment. The trouble was that, although Paris *haute couture* and the highest priced ready-mades were unrivalled anywhere, the cheaper chainstore clothes seemed to her definitely inferior to their British equivalents. In England, on the salary Adam paid her, she could have dressed very well, but in Paris there was simply no point in competing.

'We will go shopping at lunchtime,' Nicole said brightly. 'I know some boutiques where the quality is very good and the prices quite reasonable.'

Francesca thanked her warmly. She pinned her hopes on Nicole's boutiques, but decided, all the same, to break her métro journey home at the Boulevard Haussmann, to see whether the two big department stores had anything suitable. A hectic hour-long search, however, failed to turn up anything that was quite right.

She got back to her room at seven o'clock, hot and footsore. She splashed cold water on her face, then, pulling open her wardrobe and drawers, piled all her clothes out on the bed.

In increasing desperation she attempted to arrange them in suitable combinations, but nothing satisfied her. Even her favourites looked either dull or shabby. 'Whatever is the matter with you? Do you seriously think you have a chance of outshining Gabrielle de Montbel?' she asked herself crossly.

She sank back on the bed in exhaustion and was still there when the landlady knocked at the door and opened it.

'Oh, Mam'selle, you are unwell?'

'No, Madame. I was just — sorting things out,' Francesca said lamely.

Madame Bauchet held a letter out to her. 'A letter came for you, Mademoiselle. I did not hear you come in at your usual time.'

'No, I was late.' She took the proffered letter and saw it was from an old schoolfriend. 'Thank you, Madame. I'm very sorry you had to walk upstairs.'

'It's nothing.' Madame Bauchet hesitated.

Nothing her hesitation, and wanting another source of advice, Francesca told her that she was invited, with her employer, to dine with a lady who lived in Passy.

'Passy. That is very smart. Who is the lady?'

'She is called Gabrielle de Montbel.'

'But I know her name. Always she is in the fashion pages and the society columns. Come, we will look in some magazines and see what the lady wears.'

In the wake of the landlady's ample figure, Francesca went downstairs. The news of Gabrielle's dominance of the fashion scene depressed her even further, but Madame Bauchet was quivering with excitement.

In the living-room, she dived into a

low cupboard and emerged with an armful of magazines which she began to leaf through eagerly. After a few minutes, she gave a cry of triumph. 'Here, you see! '*Gabrielle de Montbel, glittering socialite, arriving at the opera*'. And look — here is your Monsieur Preston. I thought the night he brought you here that I had seen him before. Oh, he is handsome, that one!'

★　★　★

Francesca took the magazine and looked at the picture Madame Bauchet indicated. Gabrielle was in a group in the foyer of the opera. She wore a cloak of stiff satin and her hair was confined in a delicate filigree of gold mesh. She looked quite simply breathtaking. She was on Adam's arm and his head was bent attentively towards her.

While Francesca looked, Madame Bauchet had been finding further pictures. Gabrielle at the races, at a charity ball, riding in the Bois du Boulogne. Seven photographs in all, and in four of them she had been squired by Adam.

Francesca said, 'I don't see any of Monsieur de Montbel.'

Madame Bauchet scrutinised the photographs. '*Non*. It seems that Monsieur Preston is Madame's escort,' she said matter-of-factly.

Francesca cleared her throat. 'I wonder why that is. I don't think she's a widow. Celestine mentioned her husband.'

The landlady's shrug conveyed a wealth of meaning. 'Who can say? But Monsieur Preston is received at her house, Mademoiselle.'

Francesca took her point. Even in France it was unlikely that a man would welcome his wife's lover in his home.

After half-an-hour of chat, and not very useful advice, Francesca returned to her room, little comforted. The sheer magnificence of Gabrielle's social life shook her, as, for some reason, did

Adam's devoted attendance.

She replaced all her clothes, made herself coffee and a sandwich, and decided on an early night.

As Nicole had promised, the next two lunchtimes were devoted to a tour of likely boutiques, but, at the end of the time, she had to admit herself beaten. Nothing that Francesca could possibly afford had been suitable for the occasion.

It was in a mood of near desperation that Francesca left for home on Friday evening. She was too tired and dispirited to make another evening sortie into the city, but she had tomorrow off and would devote the whole day to the search.

She had not got beyond the third stair as she was going up to her room, when Madame Bauchet erupted into the hall, agog with excitement.

'Oh, Mademoiselle!' she cried. 'The box has arrived. It is the dress, is it not? May I see it?'

Francesca stared at her. 'What box? I

don't understand, Madame.'

'The dress-box, Mademoiselle. It arrived by messenger this afternoon. It is addressed to you. I will fetch it.'

Puzzled, Francesca followed Madame Bauchet into her livingroom. The dress-box reposed in the centre of the table, a dove-grey box with the legend, *Chloé*, printed in tiny maroon letters all over it, and tied with a maroon silk ribbon.

'*Chloé*,' said Madame Bauchet with a hint of reproof. 'Very expensive.'

'Well, I didn't buy it.' Francesca plucked the card from the ribbon. Without doubt, it was addressed to her. She untied the ribbon, lifted the lid, and parted the nest of dove-grey tissue.

Inside she caught the shimmer of palest green silk like the silvery underside of a leaf. Very gently she drew the dress from the box. It was beautifully cut, with a narrow pleated frill at the hem and a subtle crossover effect at the bust. It was exactly what she had been looking for and never, in a million years, expected to find.

She said, 'It's absolutely perfect.'

'It's beautiful, quite beautiful,' Madame Bauchet breathed. 'Such quality, such *chic*.' Then, practically, 'But will it fit?'

'Oh, please God,' Francesca prayed.

She pushed the dress back into the box and flew up the stairs to her room. Once inside, she pulled off her blouse and skirt and slipped the dress over her head with trembling hands. She smoothed down her hair and approached the mirror. Her image delighted her. The dress fitted perfectly. It set off her colouring and it suggested a genuine, though youthful sophistication.

★　★　★

Turning away, well pleased, she noticed an envelope half-hidden among the wrapping in the box. She tore it open and read the message, in Adam's handwriting. '*I thought you might have little time or opportunity to shop for an outfit for Sunday,*' it ran. '*I hope you will accept this from me. I feel the firm is somewhat in your debt as you were so underpaid in Lynford. If the dress is not to your taste, the shop will be happy to change it. I look forward to our excursion. Until Sunday, Adam.'*

As she read the brief letter, Francesca was touched by the sensitivity that had gone into it. In the few lines, Adam had supplied her pride with two let-outs. In implying that she would only be without a suitable dress because she hadn't had the time or opportunity to buy one, and in suggesting that he owed her the cost of the dress in back wages.

And, in his busy schedule, to have thought of the purchase of the dress at all, and to have chosen something that suited her and fitted her so well, showed an understanding that she could not deny. She wished that their relationship was such that she could have rushed to the phone and poured out her gratitude to him, but she resolved to be impeccably mannered on Sunday night.

After modelling the dress for an admiring Madame Bauchet, she hung it up carefully and went out for a quick supper at a nearby café, revelling in the knowledge that she needn't spend the next day in a frantic search.

As it was, she slept late, then had her hair washed at a very special place and invested in a pair of expensive kid pumps with the money she had saved on the dress.

On Saturday she occupied herself fairly well, but Sunday seemed endless, with the butterflies in her stomach increasing hourly.

At six o'clock she started on her make-up, an operation which never normally took her more than ten minutes, then donned the dress, her sheerest tights and the new shoes. When, at last, she heard the faint ring of the doorbell at seven o'clock, she was satisfied with her appearance, but a quivering mass of nerves inside.

She descended the stairs to find Adam waiting for her. He was wearing a dinner suit which quite unfairly enhanced his attraction, the snowy shirt accentuating his tan.

He smiled down at her. 'You look enchanting.'

Francesca flushed. 'It's largely your doing. Thank you so much for the dress.'

'It's not my doing at all. You're too modest. The dress simply sets off your appeal.'

He led her out to the car, handed her in, and they slid away from the kerb.

'Will there be many people there?' Francesca asked nervously.

'I don't imagine so. The de Montbels only entertain small parties at home. Probably six or eight. You'll like Gaston. He's one of my oldest friends.'

The streets of Paris were fairly quiet on a Sunday evening as they turned towards the Seine. Stealing a glance at Adam — the incredibly deep blue eyes beneath quizzical brows, the long, enigmatic mouth — Francesca found herself wishing that they were not bound for Gabrielle's house, but could drive together through the night in this little intimate enclosure. Hastily, she thrust the thought from her.

They drove in silence until they came to a cul-de-sac of large houses. Adam stopped behind another car. Recognising it, he smiled at Francesca reassuringly. 'Doctor Ricard is here. He doesn't eat little English girls, I promise you.'

He took her icy hand and led her to the front door. At Adam's ring, a uniformed maid opened the door to a large, sumptuously furnished hall.

A second later Gabrielle hurried out to greet them. She kissed them both on the cheeks and stood back to appraise Francesca's appearance.

'But Francesca, you look ravishing!' she cried. 'Doesn't she look marvellous, Adam? What a clever girl to have discovered such a good *couturier* so quickly.'

She left a half-question hanging in the air, but Francesca merely murmured her thanks. Any suspicions

Gabrielle might have about the origins of the dress, she could keep. Gabrielle herself was wearing a rose-pink dress of a somewhat similar style, and Francesca was grateful, once again, to Adam for his inspired choice.

'Come in,' Gabrielle was saying. 'The Ricards are here.' She wrinkled her nose at Adam. 'A little dull, but Gaston likes to see them. And the Fourniers will be here soon.'

She ushered them into a large salon furnished in the French grand manner with a lot of marble, gilt and velvet. On the far side of the room a middle-aged couple shared a small sofa and, beside them, sat a markedly handsome man of about forty. He looked up as they approached. He bore a slight resemblance to Adam, but his body was more powerfully built and his dark hair was greying at the temples. He did not get to his feet at his guests' approach, although Doctor Ricard had risen and bowed over Francesca's hand.

Hesitantly, Francesca extended her

hand and, still seated, Gaston de Montbel kissed it.

'A thousand pardons that I cannot rise to greet you, Mademoiselle,' he said. He made a slight gesture and, looking down, Francesca saw wheels beneath his chair.

'I'm sorry, Monsieur,' Francesca stumbled.

'And I also, Mademoiselle, but that is an old story. Come, sit by me and tell me how this dreadful fellow is treating you.'

Doctor Ricard, a plump and prosperous-looking man with black-rimmed spectacles, vacated his seat and began to talk to Adam. He was joined by his wife, a dark, heavily made-up woman in an unflattering string-coloured gown.

'I don't see very much of Adam,' Francesca said.

'A diplomatic answer. Do you enjoy working at the Lute?'

'Very much. I feel an affinity with the old scholars and the University. There is such atmosphere — ' Francesca found herself talking freely. Conversation with Gaston de Montbel was amazingly easy. He gave her his complete attention, as though he had been waiting all day just to hear her opinions.

After about ten minutes the doorbell was heard and, in a moment, the two remaining guests appeared in the doorway. The man and woman were both around thirty. The man, conservatively dressed, had blond hair, cut rather long. The woman, intensely thin, with her hair dragged into a knot on top of her head and an exotic style of make-up, wore a purple silk trousersuit with feather trimmings. She rushed across the room to Adam and Gabrielle, embracing them warmly and uttering loud endearments, then catapulted on to Gaston.

Disentangling himself from her embrace, Gaston introduced her to Francesca as Sylvie Fournier.

'I am so happy to meet you,' Sylvie exclaimed. 'Gabrielle telephoned me to say I must meet Adam's English girl and I think, 'Oh, a frump!' But, *non*, not a frump, *pas de tout*. Tell me, *chérie*, where did you get that enchanting dress? For me, I think, too quiet, but for *L'Anglaise*, it is perfect.'

The new guest rattled on in a strong Parisian accent, while her husband quietly introduced himself as Philippe Fournier.

As Sylvie did not seem to expect any response to her conversation, Francesca was again spared embarrassment over the source of the dress. They talked for a few more minutes before the maid came in to announce dinner and Gabrielle led the way through the hall to the dining-room.

* * *

The dining-room was smaller than the reception room, but furnished with the same taste and luxury. It had panelled walls and deep red curtains that gave it a warm intimate air. The big circular dining-table was beautifully set and lit by candles backed by the soft glow from two standing lamps.

Gaston steered his wheelchair into a chairless space, and Gabrielle placed her guests. Francesca was seated between Gaston and Doctor Ricard, with Adam directly across the table from her, between Gabrielle and Sylvie. As soon as they were settled, two uniformed maids began to serve them.

It was a superb meal. As course followed delicious course, each accompanied by its appropriate wine, Francesca began to relax and enjoy herself.

The conversation was dominated by Sylvie, who kept up a non-stop flow of chatter, helped out by Adam and Gabrielle.

When the meal was over, the party returned to the salon. Francesca found herself cornered by Sylvie who turned to her and enquired, in English, in clear carrying tones, 'And what is between you and Adam, *chérie? Une affaire?*'

Francesca felt herself blushing scarlet. She attempted to explain, in a very low voice, that it was nothing but an employer/employee relationship, but Sylvie was not convinced.

'But he takes you out to dinner, *non?* Does he escort the worthy Nicole, or — what is her name — Ernestine?'

'Celestine.' Gabrielle's voice was cold. 'Of course he doesn't. Don't be an idiot, Sylvie. Francesca was a stranger, alone in Paris, and I suggested to Adam that he brought her along for dinner.'

It sounded uncomfortably like an act of charity to Francesca and must have done so to Sylvie, for she rounded on Gabrielle.

'*Oh, la, la!* No man in his right mind would regard escorting Francesca as a chore.' She turned back to Francesca. 'He is considered a great catch, that one. The most eligible bachelor in Paris, wouldn't you say, Gaby?' She looked archly at her hostess. 'That is, if he could be called eligible!'

Francesca was in agony lest Sylvie's words had carried to Adam. She shot a swift look at him. He was leaning against the ornate marble mantelpiece, his lean figure inclined over Gaston's chair, ostensibly listening to him, but from the sardonic smile that played across his wry mouth, she suspected that he had caught the drift of their conversation.

As she prayed fervently that some fresh subject would engage Sylvie's interest, Gabrielle stalked across the room and put some music on the stereo. As the strains floated out, Philippe pulled his wife to her feet, clutched her to him and danced away. Gabrielle turned to Adam, slipped into his arms, and they joined Sylvie and Philippe. Doctor Ricard had returned to his wife and together they watched the dancers. Gaston caught Francesca's eye and smiled ruefully. He sped his chair smoothly across the room to her side.

He nodded at the dancers. 'I regret that we cannot join the others, mademoiselle.'

'I'm much too full up to dance,'

Francesca assured him quickly.

'Perhaps you would like a tour of inspection? I'm something of a collector and I think you would appreciate some of my *objets*.'

Francesca agreed willingly and followed Gaston around the salon as he told her about various pieces. It was obvious that he was a keen collector and he was knowledgeable about his treasures. They drifted into the hall and Gaston was showing her a collection of Limoges china, when the music from the salon grew louder and more disruptive. Francesca glanced in and saw that Sylvie appeared to be demonstrating some uninhibited new step, but Adam and Gabrielle still danced close in each other's arms. Francesca glanced involuntarily at Gaston. He was quite expressionless as he carefully replaced an exquisite gilded box, painted with a miniature pastoral scene.

He said quietly, 'I did not expect my wife's life to end with mine, mademoiselle.'

Francesca flushed. 'I intended no judgment, monsieur.'

'I'm sure you didn't. And, in any case, I was being melodramatic. My life is, by no means, ended. I have many interests and pleasures, and chief of them is my wife. It gives me happiness to see her happy, and she needs to lead a full social life. Now, shall we return to the others? Perhaps you would like to dance, too?'

'Oh, no. I've so much enjoyed looking at your lovely things,' Francesca said.

'It has delighted me to show them to you. But you have not seen a half. You must come again. Perhaps you would be interested in my library? I have several fine things that Adam has found for me.'

Francesca assured him that she would, and, together, they returned to the salon.

★　★　★

The music had just stopped, and Adam left Gabrielle and joined Francesca. He smiled down at her, his perfect teeth white against his tanned skin.

'Would you care to dance, Francesca?'

'No, thank you.'

Adam looked after Gaston, who was propelling himself towards his wife. 'It won't hurt Gaston's feelings, or anything like that, you know. In fact, he dislikes people being overtactful.'

'I wasn't thinking of Monsieur de Montbel's feelings. I simply don't feel like dancing.'

And most certainly not with you, she thought to herself. Not when his mere proximity was making her heart race so uncomfortably.

'Don't be such a little prig.' The strains of a romantic ballad swept across the room and she was pulled roughly into his arms. Francesca gasped. Pressed against the length of his lean body, his cheek against her hair, she felt such a rush of powerful emotion that she thought she would faint. Her heart thudded in her ears and her legs seemed to turn to jelly. She was horrified at the strength of her feelings. 'I must leave', she thought desperately. 'I must get out of here and I must leave Paris. I can't fight him.'

'Relax,' he murmured into her hair. 'Let yourself go.' And somehow, miraculously, she did. He was such a superb dancer that she found herself moving smoothly about the floor, part of him, and part of the music, and she couldn't bear it ever to end.

As the poignant tune drew to a close, he leant back a little and touched her gently under the chin so that she lifted her head and their eyes locked. His other hand burned into the small of her back.

'Have you enjoyed your evening, little one?'

Francesca swallowed hard. Why did 'little one' seem to mean so much more than *petite* which was heard on every hand?

The music stopped and the magic with it. She slid out of his arms and it was like leaving paradise. 'I've had a wonderful time,' she said huskily. 'A marvellous meal, and Monsieur de Montbel was so kind.'

'Oh, yes. A very understanding man, Gaston.'

The Fourniers had stopped dancing and a maid appeared with a tray of drinks. Sylvie, as vivacious as when she first arrived, was pressing Gabrielle and Adam to make up a foursome to ride in the Bois the following afternoon.

Adam accepted, but Gabrielle said crossly, 'You know perfectly well, Sylvie, that I have my tennis lesson on a Monday afternoon.'

'Oh, *tiens!* It had slipped my mind.' Sylvie turned to Francesca. 'What about you, *chérie?* Do you ride?'

Francesca had no intention of being foisted on a reluctant Adam again. She shook her head firmly. 'It's kind of you, but I have to work tomorrow.'

'But Adam is your boss, no? So you twiddle the boss round your little finger!'

'I think she could manage that,' Adam said cryptically.

Sylvie swung round on him. 'Then you give her the afternoon off — for the fresh air? And she must see our beautiful Bois.'

Adam smiled. 'How about it, Francesca? I don't think she's going to take no for an answer. You do ride, don't you?'

'A little. But I have no riding clothes with me.'

'But I can lend them. I will send everything you need over to the Lute in the morning.' Sylvie surveyed her emaciated form with satisfaction. 'You are not so slim as I, but I think you can get into my clothes.'

Gabrielle was looking far from pleased at the turn events had taken, but she rallied herself and talked charmingly to her guests until, at eleven o'clock, Adam and Francesca left.

★ ★ ★

107

As they headed back for the centre of Paris, Adam said, 'Would you like to go on somewhere else?'

'At eleven o'clock on a Sunday night? Where could we go?'

'You seem to persist in regarding Paris as a second Lynford. Where would you like to go? Cabaret, a supper club, a disco, *le jazz*?'

The temptation was almost too strong to resist. But some last remnant of good sense told her that to be alone with him was fraught with danger — alluring as the prospect might be.

She said, 'I'm afraid I've been a Lynford girl too long! I've had enough excitement for one night.'

'So — home to bed?'

'Yes, please.'

As they drove up the Rue des Martyrs, Francesca said, tentatively, 'I seem to have been wished on you once again.'

He shrugged lightly. 'Well, as I said before, it looks as if we're stuck with each other. It wasn't too bad, was it?'

'Tonight was wonderful. But tomorrow — my riding really is very rusty, you know.'

'I'll see that you get a docile mount.'

'It was kind of Madame Fournier to invite me, and to lend me a riding habit.'

She thought he smiled in the darkness. 'Sylvie's motives are usually somewhat complex.'

Puzzled by the odd reply, she ventured, 'She's very entertaining.'

'Yes, she was beginning to do well in her profession when she married Philippe.'

'Her profession?'

'She was an actress. Mainly television comedy.'

'I should imagine she'd be very good. Has she given it up?'

He looked mildly shocked. 'Of course. The Fourniers are a very distinguished family. It was bad enough that Philippe married someone like Sylvie — '

'Why on earth shouldn't he?'

'Well, in France it's still expected that a woman will bring a comparable pedigree — or at least, wealth — to a marriage. But the minute Philippe met Sylvie, he fell hook, line and sinker, and any thought of a marriage settlement went completely out of his head.'

'So I should think!' Francesca was indignant. 'What a dreadfully calculating attitude to marriage!'

'Not at all. It's very practical. It safeguards the family name and property. In any event, it seems to work — divorce and promiscuity are less common here.'

'I thought France was the land of the mistress.'

'That, too, is a practical arrangement to safeguard the family.' The car crossed the square and came to a stop outside Madame Bauchets'. 'However, I have to admit, in the Fournier's case, it seems to have been a success, so far. They have been married for three years and they are still besotted with each other.'

His tone was reluctant, and Francesca

felt sure that he personally subscribed to the more businesslike arrangement. Love at first sight, with a nobody who could bring neither money nor acceptable family connections to the match, would not be for him.

He got out of the car and escorted her to the front door and said goodnight, making no suggestions that he should come further, and Francesca walked upstairs feeling oddly depressed. He had taken himself off with unflattering readiness, she reflected ruefully, just as he had immediately accepted her reluctance to prolong the evening on the town. Not that she had wanted it otherwise — his effect on her self-control seemed to be disastrous — but she would have liked the chance to refuse. As for his attitude to marriage, that should have come as no surprise. She had witnessed his cold-blooded approach to both business and personal relationships in his dealings with his uncle.

If she had any sense, she told herself

as she prepared for bed, hanging up the lovely dress carefully, she would use Adam Preston as she had originally planned. Tonight she had enjoyed a pleasant evening and met some interesting people. There was no reason why there should not be other evenings to her advantage. But why, oh why, she thought, as her throbbing head touched the pillow, was it so difficult to remember her plan whenever she was close to him?

★   ★   ★

She slept later than usual the following morning. The sun that usually bathed her room was absent and, when she drew back the curtains, she was faced with a sullen grey sky, although it was still very warm. As she showered and dressed, she couldn't decide whether or not she hoped that the threatened downpour would wash out the afternoon's expedition.

She set off at a brisk trot towards the

métro station, feeling headachy and slightly sick, for which she blamed a combination of the rich food and wine she had consumed at Gabrielle's, and apprehension about the coming outing.

At ten o'clock, as she was telling Nicole and Celestine about the previous evening, a uniformed chauffeur delivered a box containing the borrowed riding clothes.

Francesca felt even sicker as she opened the box and saw the smart habit. The afternoon outing, which she had almost succeeded in pushing to the back of her mind, now seemed inevitable. Watched by the two women, she lifted out a beautifully-cut black hacking jacket, cream jodhpurs, a snowy white shirt and stock, shiny black riding boots and a black bowler hat. Laughing excitedly, Celestine slipped the jacket over Francesca's dress and tilted the bowler on her head at a rakish angle.

'*Tiens!* It is not the chorus of the Moulin Rouge!' Nicole chided. She straightened the hat. 'That is the way. You look beautiful, *ma petite*. You have the true English *chic*.'

Francesca sat down heavily on a packing case. 'Perhaps the boots won't fit,' she said hopefully.

Challenged, Celestine began to push them on and Francesca was still seated on the packing case wearing the hat and jacket, booted legs stretched out below her cotton dress, when Adam erupted into the room.

'Is there anyone in this place?' he demanded sharply. 'Nicole, Marcel has been looking for you for ten minutes — ' He broke off, seeing Francesca, and she thought for a moment that a smile twitched at his mobile mouth. 'Francesca, do you think the fancy dress might wait for a more suitable occasion?'

She got to her feet, painfully conscious of what an idiot she must look. 'I'm sorry. It was my fault. The riding clothes that Madame Fournier is lending me just arrived and I thought I had better try them on — ' She subsided back on to her packing case and looked around for Celestine to help her remove the boots, but both women had disappeared upon Adam's arrival, and she was forced to struggle with them on her own.

After watching her pulling ineffectively with the stiff straps and buckles for a minute, Adam exclaimed irritably, 'Oh, let me!'

He knelt in front of her and expertly began to unfasten the buckles, then he grasped her slim leg and slid the boot off. As he repeated the process, Francesca, looking down at his dark head, felt a choking sensation in her throat. Her whole body was rigid with tension. As the second boot came off, she got quickly to her feet.

'Thank you. And I apologise for the upheaval.'

He shrugged slightly, as though upheaval was the least he expected from her. 'That's OK. Can you be ready for two o'clock?'

'Any time you say.'

'Right.'

★ ★ ★

Francesca watched him go, her heart racing nervously. She was going to make a fool of herself this afternoon, she was convinced.

She re-packed the box of garments and got on with her neglected work. She did without her coffee-break and got back from lunch at a nearby restaurant at one-thirty, when she closeted herself in the cloakroom and donned the riding habit. Wearing the complete outfit and with her hair, beneath the hat, brushed back and tied with a ribbon, she had to admit the effect was most flattering.

Just before two o'clock she heard Adam's voice in the shop, and she emerged and descended the stairs self-consciously. He was wearing a dark brown hacking jacket, with a tan cap and breeches, and looked extremely attractive. He raised his crop to her in a lazy salute.

'Very becoming.'

'Thank you. I only hope I can live up to the clothes.'

They went outside and Francesca saw that the sky was now a leaden grey all over. Scarcely a breath of air seemed to move. Adam opened the car door. Inside it was baking hot.

'Phew!' She tugged at the tight stock at her throat. 'Do you think it will rain soon?'

'It feels like it. Why? I didn't think English roses minded a little rain.'

Francesca thought the jibe beneath her notice and ignored him.

'Where are we meeting the Fourniers?' she enquired after a few minutes.

'At the stables, inside the park.'

'Is Madame Fournier a good rider?'

Adam shrugged slightly. 'I've no idea. I've never ridden with her. Her invitation last night came as a complete surprise to me.'

'Well — I suppose the invitation was

to Madame de Montbel, really.'

'Do you think so?' He shot her a curious glance, but, before she could respond, they had entered the park.

A minute later, he stopped in front of an extremely smart livery stable. It was a long, low, chalet-like building, with neatly clipped trees in tubs along the façade. A group of people attired in elegant riding dress, some mounted, some on foot, laughed and talked together in the forecourt.

Adam said, 'I don't see Philippe or Sylvie anywhere. Let's go and see about our mounts, maybe they're around the back.'

He parked the car under a clump of trees and strode round to the back of the building with Francesca scurrying at his heels.

A pretty girl groom approached them with a message. Francesca caught the words *téléphone* and *la migraine* and her heart sank, particularly when she saw the scowl on Adam's face. The girl returned to her duties and Adam turned to Francesca.

'No doubt you'll be amazed to hear that Sylvie has called off? A convenient headache apparently.'

Bewildered at his tone, she said doubtfully, 'I'm sorry. I expect it's the oppressive weather.'

'Don't tell me you really expected them to be here? It's patently obvious to me that it was just a piece of mischief on Sylvie's part.'

'I don't seem to follow what you're getting at — '

'Oh, come now, you can do better than that. Surely you realise it was nothing but a stupid, childish ploy to throw us together?'

4

Blazing with anger, Francesca flushed a deep scarlet. Momentarily bereft of words, she spluttered, 'If what you say is true — and as I fail to see that it's such a thrill for me to be 'thrown together' with you — I would say it was I who had been made a fool of by your friends. And if you think I was involved in the stupid plot, may I remind you that I had never met Madame Fournier before last night?'

He had the grace to look a little dubious. 'There's always been a bit of a needle match between Sylvie and Gabrielle,' he muttered. 'And Sylvie has plenty of surplus energy to expend on her little machinations — '

'I don't want to ride, anyway,' Francesca broke in. 'It's going to pour at any minute, so you can take me back to work.' She turned on her heel and started back towards the car.

'No, wait, Francesca!' He hurried after her and caught her by the arm. 'I'm sorry if I was rude. It's just that I hate to be made a fool of, especially by — '

'Especially by a conniving woman?'

She could see that her remark had struck home, but he pressed on. 'We might as well ride, now we're here. I could do with the fresh air and you look as though you could too.'

Francesca hesitated. Part of her longed to ride with him, the other part was a churning mixture of nerves and anger.

'Well,' she said. 'If they have a very quiet horse — '

'Sidonie!' Adam called to the girl who had delivered Sylvie's message. '*Un cheval très tranquille pour made-moiselle.*'

They conferred together for a minute, then Adam said to Francesca, 'She suggests Caramel, the little bay mare. The Comtesse Dupuy always rides her and she is nearly eighty.'

Taking this as a reasonable guarantee, Francesca walked over to the horse he indicated. 'She's a darling,' she said, caressing the glossy neck. The stable-girl got the horse out and helped Francesca to saddle up. Meanwhile, Adam saddled his own mount, a big black by the name of Sabre.

The rich sweetish smell of horse and hay intoxicated Francesca and she began to look forward to the ride. She had enjoyed the riding she had done as a schoolgirl and, as she mounted and followed Adam out of the yard, the technique automatically returned to her.

They walked the horses carefully across the road and set off at a gentle canter over a wide stretch of parkland. The motion and the rush of air exhilarated Francesca and she turned her face up in pleasure. As she did so, a large raindrop hit her nose.

Damn, she thought, annoyed. But Adam didn't seem to have noticed it, and she certainly wasn't going to be the one to cry off at the first drop of rain.

Besides, she was enjoying herself too much.

At the far side of the open land, a narrow bridle path led between thin clumps of trees and they slowed to a walk. Sabre was acting skittishly, tossing his neck and rolling his eyes, and was obviously not an easy horse to control, but Caramel behaved impeccably.

'Here begins the forest proper,' Adam said. 'It was the royal hunting-ground of the Valois kings. Do you want to go any further?'

'Oh, yes!' Francesca's cheeks were pink and her eyes sparkled. Adam turned away quickly before she could see the admiration in his own.

★ ★ ★

They followed the bridle path deeper into the wood; sycamores, chestnuts and acacia began to engulf them as the path grew narrower. Francesca could imagine that, on a bright day, sunlight might filter down between the trees, but

123

today the wood was dark and a steady tattoo of raindrops had started to rattle on to the leaves. Once or twice, Sabre's great flank nudged Caramel, and Francesca felt a tremor go through her horse.

'Blast it! Here comes the rain,' Adam said. 'I was hoping we'd get back before it started. We'd better stay under the trees.'

They reined in for a moment in a leafy glade. The rain was obviously heavy outside the cover of the trees, but here only the occasional spot reached them. From far off came the first distant rumble of thunder and Caramel twitched more violently. A second later, a shattering peal of thunder crashed directly overhead. Caramel gave a high whinnying squeal and, with a lurch that almost dislocated Francesca's spine, took off at a fast swerving gallop between the trees.

Francesca heard Adam's voice, in sudden alarm, shouting, 'Hold her, hold her!' as she fought to control her horse, then the earth-shaking pounding of Sabre's hoofs behind her, at which Caramel laid back her ears and redoubled her speed. The horse swerved sharply to avoid a low branch and Francesca sailed through the air to land with a bone-jarring crunch on the ground.

Her hat had stayed on and taken most of the impact, but she felt sick and shaky as she tried to sit up. Adam had dismounted and knelt beside her, his face white with concern.

'Are you all right?' he asked urgently.

'I think so.' She shook her head cautiously and was rewarded by a wave of nausea. She rested her head against the tree behind her. 'My horse — I must catch her,' she said weakly.

'She'll find her way back.' His look of concern changed to irritation. 'But couldn't you control her? I thought you said you could ride!'

'I could have controlled her — ' she bit off her words icily — 'if you hadn't come crashing up on that — that great brute. He's been making her nervous all afternoon — rolling his eyes at her!'

'He's a gelding, so he's not likely to have designs on her. Are you going to recline there all afternoon, or can you stand up?'

He put an arm round her waist and she got to her feet. Every bone in her body ached, and one ankle was very painful when she put her foot to the ground.

She winced. 'I don't think I can walk all the way back.'

'You can ride up with me, but we'll have to shelter for a while — it's still pouring.'

The rain was indeed drumming down into the open glade where they stood. Adam pulled Francesca into the shelter of an enormous horse chestnut tree. She looked down at her clothes aghast. The cream jodhpurs were covered in mud and there were streaks on the jacket.

'Adam, look at my clothes!' Her eyes filled with tears. 'Whatever will Sylvie say?'

'Oh, lord, it doesn't matter. I suppose you couldn't help it. They'll clean, and if they don't, I'll replace them.'

'I don't want you making a habit of buying my clothes,' she said primly. She had pulled out of his restraining arm and was supporting herself against the tree, when another deafening clap of thunder, directly overhead, made her jump and almost stumble.

'I think we'd better get out from under here,' Adam said. 'I seem to remember a kiosk out in the open at the end of this path. Lean on me and we'll make a run for it.'

★   ★   ★

He put his arm tightly round her waist and she was forced to do the same with him. They started off at an awkward jog along the bridle path. At the edge of the wood they stopped, and Adam peered out through the blinding rain. 'Yes, there it is.'

About a hundred yards away, Francesca

saw an old-fashioned kiosk of the sort that is seen all over Paris. It looked extremely small.

She said doubtfully, 'Couldn't we stay here?'

She was answered by another shattering crack of thunder. Before she knew what he was doing, Adam bent down, put his other arm beneath her knees and swept her up into his arms. She gasped, but there was simply no point in arguing at such a time. She put her head down against his chest, conscious of its hard muscles and the strength of his arms. He bent his head over hers protectively and hurried forward through the rain.

They reached the kiosk, Adam kicked open the door, and they tumbled inside. They found themselves in a tiny hexagonal room, almost dark, very warm and smelling of damp. Panting heavily, Adam stripped off his soaking wet jacket and cap, then turned to Francesca. She was leaning heavily against the wall, her face white with pain, her garments dripping water.

She said, 'I'm sorry, it's all my fault — ' Against her will, tears welled in her eyes.

'Now stop that! The storm wasn't your fault — it was stupid to start out. And if you're worried about your horse, look outside!'

She pushed the door open and looked out. Sabre, who had followed them to the kiosk, was grazing nearby, and Francesca's mare trotted eagerly towards him.

'She seems to have overcome her fears!' Adam said drily.

Francesca laughed in relief, a laugh that somehow turned into a sob. As she did so, Adam's hands reached out towards her body. She watched them in fascinated horror, longing for his touch and yet dreading it. Then he began to undo the buttons of her coat.

'Better get that off, you're soaking.' His voice was husky. Francesca let out her pent up breath. He helped her off with her jacket and tossed her hat after it. He dabbed her face with his handkerchief, then attempted to dry her dripping little ponytail of hair.

Suddenly she was terribly aware of him in the close warm darkness. Less than two feet separated them, and she pressed back against the wall, her heart racing. She pushed his hands away. 'It's all right. It will soon dry.'

He put his hands on her shoulders, feeling the damp silk of her shirt. 'I don't want you to catch pneumonia.'

At the touch of his warm hands she started to tremble, her whole body yearned for contact with his, yet she despised herself for the longing. She strove to remember the hatred that had brought her to Paris, but the memory dissolved in her vulnerability and longing. Adam's hands slid down her arms, and his eyes, dark and unfathomable, looked down into hers. Slowly he pulled her to him and his mouth, gently questing, came down on hers.

For a moment his mouth was soft on her parted lips, then his grip began to tighten like steel bands on her upper arms. His mouth grew more insistent, claiming hers relentlessly until she almost cried out in pain. Then one hand moved to caress her breast through the damp clinging silk. She felt the urgency in him and he began to tremble, almost out of control.

She began to struggle, beating against his chest with frenzied fists. 'No, Adam. No!'

For a moment he was oblivious to her protest, consumed by blind desire, then he gave a shudder and almost thrust her from him. In his eyes desire slowly changed to distaste. He leant back against the wall behind him, smoothing his hair with a hand that trembled slightly.

★ ★ ★

'You little witch,' he said softly. 'I should have been prepared for your magic.'

'What do you mean?' Francesca

paused in straightening her shirt and stared at him. 'Adam, I swear I didn't want this — '

'Oh, don't lie! Although I admit you're very good. It's easy to see how you bewitched my uncle, when I almost fell under your spell.'

Her cheeks flamed. 'I've told you there was nothing like that between your uncle and me. If that's the only kind of relationship you can imagine, your mind's diseased!'

She was shaking with anger, cold and the residue of the tension that had built up in her body. She grabbed her hat and jacket and pushed open the door. 'I'm going.'

'Don't be an idiot. Do you want to be struck by lightning?'

She struggled into the wet jacket and clamped the hat on her head. 'It would be preferable to staying here with you,' she announced icily.

She squelched across grass that had been churned into a morass by the intensity of the downpour. The rain had now eased off somewhat and the thunder rumbled away in the distance.

To her intense relief, Caramel allowed her to approach and catch the rein. She climbed into the sodden saddle.

Adam had followed her, his jacket in his hand. He swung himself lightly up on to Sabre's back.

'And, incidentally, I'm giving in my notice!' Francesca informed him.

He gave a smile that was far from pleasant. 'Very well. But don't forget you must work out a month's notice. It's in your contract.'

He dug in his heels and set off at a furious gallop, throwing up clods of mud as his horse wheeled round.

Francesca followed at a more sober pace. As long as she kept him in sight, that was quite enough. His proximity had been her undoing. She burned with shame as she recalled the surrender he must have sensed in her, and groaned inwardly. No wonder he had thought her promiscuous if she fell into his arms so eagerly at the first opportunity.

By the time she reached the stables Adam had unsaddled his horse and was supervising his rubbing-down. He helped her down and handed Caramel over to a second groom.

To Francesca, he said, 'Get in the car, I'll take you home.'

She did as he said, huddling as far away from him as she could get, and they drove to Montmartre in silence. It was only sensible that he should take her home — there was no way she could have got dry at the shop — and yet she felt that he only desired to have her off his hands.

At her destination she got out of the car without a word and, slamming the door behind her, stalked to her front door and disappeared inside. She hurried upstairs, relieved to meet no one on the way. Her wet clothes were profoundly uncomfortable by now, and she stripped them off into a soggy pile on the floor and put on her dressing-gown.

There was no gainsaying that the

afternoon had been a total disaster. She had revealed her feelings to Adam, and he had humiliated and insulted her. Sylvie Fournier's expensive clothes were ruined, and she was probably out of a job. Feeling very sorry for herself, she trailed along to the bathroom where she washed her hair and soaked herself for a long time in the enormous tub.

When she emerged, she felt somewhat restored. In her room she found some bread and cheese, made herself a pot of coffee, and sat at her window, looking out over the city as she ate.

★   ★   ★

It seemed to her that, with Adam, there had been an inexplicable turning of the tables, as though the ground had moved beneath her feet in some way. She had come to Paris with a clear and unmistakeable grievance against him, but, right from the start, he had behaved as though she was the culpable one.

The only course open to her was to leave his employ. The effect that his presence had on her made it impossible for her to continue at the Silver Lute. But perhaps she could find another job in Paris. Her French had greatly improved and there was nothing for her to return to in Lynford. With that thought in mind, she did a few chores, including washing Sylvie's shirt, and went early to bed.

She had retired so early that she woke before seven the following morning. As she took her shower, she noticed that a number of bruises from her fall had appeared on her skin, including two on her upper arms that must have come from Adam's grasp. At the memory of that tormenting moment, her body seemed to melt, but she pulled herself together angrily. Somehow the month had to be got through with no further degrading weakness.

She gave the riding jacket, boots and hat a vigorous brushing that returned them to something like their original condition, ironed the shirt, and packed them all in a box. The jodhpurs would have to be taken to the local cleaners. Then she changed into a becoming yellow linen suit, and applied a little make-up. She had been asked to lunch by a customer, a charming elderly American, and she wanted to be a credit to him.

She arrived at the shop a moment behind Adam. He coloured slightly when he saw her, then said, 'Good morning. No ill effects after yesterday, I hope?'

'None whatever,' Francesca replied shortly. 'I'm returning Madame Fournier's clothes. Perhaps you could see that they get back to her. The jodhpurs are being cleaned.'

He took the box from her. She thought he was about to say something, but she brushed past him and ran upstairs to the staffroom. She worked for the first part of the morning making out invoices with Nicole, but around eleven o'clock, Marcel Vachette sent her to help Adam with some packing in the storeroom.

The books to be packed were valuable ones from the secure room, and Adam checked their insurance forms and labels, while Francesca wrapped each book carefully in thick wadding before packing it in the stout, lined box. At one point, watching her, he observed, 'I see you handle them with respect.'

She looked at him in surprise. 'I handle all books with respect and these are obviously something special.'

'They're worth a good deal of money.'

'That wasn't what I meant.'

Apart from the one remark they worked in silence, but a silence fraught with her intense awareness of his presence. She wondered why she had been detailed to do this job, anyway, which normally was entrusted to Vachette.

At just turned noon, Celestine looked round the door and sang out, 'Mam'selle, your date is waiting for you.'

Francesca had the satisfaction of

seeing Adam's head jerk round. He hesitated, then asked almost against his will, 'Who is the lucky man?'

'Professor Berger.'

'Congratulations. He's elderly, susceptible and very rich. You should get on well.'

Fury at his insinuation blazed in her once more, but she decided to ignore the jibe and leave him feeling small.

★　★　★

Lunch was delightful and very lengthy. Her companion was charming.

It was half-past-two before she returned to the shop, well-fed, well-wined and relaxed. Professor Berger bade her farewell at the door. Francesca could see Adam at the rear of the shop, watching them with a knowing smile. She said goodbye quickly and slipped inside. As she did so a second man stepped out from behind Adam.

'Still ensnaring them, I see,' he said.

'Drew!' Francesca stared, unable to

believe her eyes. But Drew it was, brightening up the shop with his close-cut golden curls, his laughing blue eyes and ready smile, a denim jacket slung casually over his sweatshirt and jeans.

'Drew,' she said again, and hurtled across the shop into his arms.

He hugged her close, kissing her warmly. 'Hey! You seem in need of a friend. Haven't they been treating you well?'

'I'm sure she'll be fine now.' Adam had been watching their reunion without expression, and Francesca slid out from Drew's embrace a little self-consciously. Pleasure at the sight of him, plus the abundance of wine at lunch, had exaggerated her reaction. It was the first time she had ever kissed him.

'It's wonderful to see you,' she said.

But Drew's hug had pushed up the sleeve of her jacket and he was staring at the ugly bruise on her arm. Gently he took her other arm and pushed up the sleeve, revealing the almost identical bruising there. 'What's this, Francesca?' he said.

The silence before she answered seemed endless. Drew looked at Adam, and Francesca, too, shot him a glance. He looked sick and shocked.

She gave a shaky laugh. 'I fell off a horse yesterday. It was nothing. I bruise ridiculously easily.'

She had the impression that all three of them released their breath. Drew still frowned slightly. It was quite obvious how the marks had been made, and it had nothing to do with a horse. He said lightly, 'You need someone to keep an eye on you. I was hoping to take you to lunch, but you were whooping it up with your old beau.'

Francesca gritted her teeth at his choice of words. Together with his initial greeting, it was exactly what was needed to confirm Adam's view of her. 'He's just a customer,' she said. 'But I can't possibly take off with you now, Drew. I've had a two-and-a-half hour lunch break, and I was out all yesterday afternoon.'

'Blast! I forgot you were a working girl.'

'Tiresome, isn't it?' Adam put in laconically. 'But do take an hour off, if you want, Francesca. After all, Drew is an old friend. And your date with Berger wasn't for pleasure — was it?'

'No, it wouldn't be fair. Perhaps after I've finished this evening, Drew.'

'Fine. I've got a room just off the Boul' Mich'. I'll call for you about six.'

With a swift peck on her cheek he was gone. Francesca watched him dash across the street, an affectionate smile on her face. When she turned back it was as if some of the sunlight had gone out of the shop. Her relationship with Drew had always been straightforward and enjoyable; now she faced this disturbing, complex man.

She said, 'I'm sorry I was so long — '

'It's all right. I realise it wasn't your fault.' He started up the stairs to his office, but stopped halfway. 'About your arms, Francesca. I'm terribly sorry. I didn't mean to hurt you. I — I seemed to lose control.'

Looking at his tight face, she could guess at the effort the apology had taken. Red with embarrassment, she said quickly: 'It's nothing, really. I turn black and blue at the slightest touch.'

They looked at each other for a long moment, and Francesca was suddenly sure that the bitter-sweet ecstasy of that moment in the kiosk was vivid in his memory, too. Then he turned and ran on up to his office.

★　★　★

She didn't see Adam again that afternoon. Drew was waiting outside for her, as he had promised, at six o'clock. They strolled up the Boulevard Saint Michel in the direction of the Luxembourg Gardens and, stopping at a café, Drew ordered coffee.

When it was brought, he said, 'So, how has it really been with you? You

143

don't look very well, and those bruises — '

'Oh, Drew, forget them! I told you how it happened. I went riding in the Bois with Adam yesterday, there was a colossal thunderstorm that spooked my horse and I came off. The whole outing was a total disaster. It poured with rain and we got soaked. I think I caught a slight chill.'

'But you like working here, with Adam?'

'I don't see a lot of him. But I love the work and I love being in Paris. How long can you stay?' Francesca added, to turn the subject away from Adam.

'Oh, until the money runs out. What do you do at the shop? Do you look after the clerical stuff as you used to do for Grandfather?'

'No, at least not much of it. I just help out generally — serving, repairing, packing.'

'What is Adam doing about the stock at the Lynford shop?'

'When he was in England last week he arranged for about half of it to be brought over here. Presumably the rest will go for auction in England.'

It seemed to her that Drew was about to say something more, but he didn't. They finished their coffee in silence, then, by unspoken consent, drifted on towards the Luxembourg Gardens which were an oasis of peace after the clamour of the boulevard.

Not long ago, Francesca thought, this would have been the summit of heaven. To be in Paris with Drew. She had always been happy in his company — to be honest she had thought herself in love with him. But meeting Adam had changed that. The feeling she had for him was quite different. Not happiness, certainly, but a mixture of rapture and pain that transformed her whole being.

And Drew was not quite as she remembered him. He was quieter and seemed almost ill-at-ease. He was making desultory conversation, and kicking at the gravel. Francesca sat down on a bench and, shading her eyes against the setting sun, regarded him with concern. After a minute she said, 'Is anything the matter, Drew?'

He came and sat down beside her, closing his eyes against the last low rays. 'What do you mean?'

'I don't know. You don't seem quite your usual bright-and-merry self.'

He shrugged slightly. 'Perhaps I've had to grow up a bit. Grandfather was the only family I had except for Adam, and I don't see much of him. It's a bit sobering to realise you're completely alone in the world.'

'Yes, it is.'

He turned to her quickly. 'I'm sorry, Fran. You've been through it, too, haven't you?'

'I'm over it now. But Drew, you must have plenty of friends.'

'I guess so.' He hesitated, then went on, 'The business of Grandfather's estate was a bit depressing — sorting out his stuff — '

'But you weren't his executor, were you? You were the heir.'

'No, Adam was his executor and

whizzed through all the business like a well-oiled automaton, needless to say. No, it was going through grandfather's personal things — having to dispose of them — '

'I'm sorry,' Francesca said softly. She put her hand over his. 'I had no idea you felt like that.'

'Oh, well,' he said vaguely. 'I suppose things will work themselves out.' He seemed to make an effort to pull himself together. 'I'm getting hungry. Are you ready to eat?'

'Yes, I am.'

$\star$ $\star$ $\star$

They hurried from the park, quite chilly now that the sun had gone, and out on to the boulevard. In the warren of side streets that led off it, they inspected menus and peered through curtained windows until they found a café to suit them, a small, clean establishment, with high-backed booths and poster-covered walls.

It was early yet, barely eight o'clock, and the place was only half-full. The *patron* brought their first course and the wine, and Drew filled their glasses, toasted Francesca, and drained his glass. He refilled it immediately and before their main course arrived he was halfway through his third glass.

Francesca was surprised and upset. It had never occurred to her that Drew was a heavy drinker. On his visits to Lynford he had drunk very moderately, and was always so fit and cheerful that she was sure it was his normal habit. This, too, was something new.

The food, substantial regional fare, was delicious, but Drew ate little, and, remembering his hearty meals when he had visited them, she was again bewildered.

When she had finished her casserole, and Drew had pushed aside the meal he had been toying with, he suddenly said, 'Francesca, do you know anything about a couple of atlases my grandfather bought not long before he died?'

Startled, she said, 'I knew he'd bought them.'

'Have you ever seen them?'

'No, they went directly into the bank, but Mr. Pinkerton used to go and gloat over them occasionally. Why?'

'I don't believe they're there any more. I keep asking Cochran to let me see them, but he just hedges. I think Adam has been putting pressure on him.'

Francesca was totally bewildered. She pushed her glass forward for a little more of the fast-diminishing wine. 'I don't understand,' she said. 'Everything at the shop is Adam's property. He has the right to keep them locked up. He was concerned about their security when he mentioned them to me. Why do you want to see them?'

'He mentioned them to you? What did he say?'

'He just wanted to know that they were safe. I believe they're extremely valuable. I told him that they were in the bank. When he returned from

149

clearing things up in Lynford, he said that he was bringing about half of Mr. Pinkerton's book stock over to Paris.'

'He didn't specify the atlases?'

'No, he didn't. Why, Drew?' she pressed.

'Because I've good reason to believe that they're not his property at all. I believe they are part of my grandfather's estate and as such they belong to me.'

She put her glass down carefully. 'Why should you think that? Are the atlases specifically mentioned in the Will?'

'No. The Will was a straightforward 'all my worldly goods'. The money in his bank account and his possessions in the flat.'

'The atlases weren't at the flat.'

'No. But they weren't at the shop, either. Think, Francesca!' He pushed his rather flushed face nearer to hers. 'Did Grandfather say anything about them when he bought them?'

'He talked of nothing else for days.

He couldn't believe they had come on the market, and then he couldn't believe he'd actually got them.'

'Would he have been so excited if he was just an agent buying on behalf of someone else?'

'He was always excited over rare or beautiful books. Of course, at that time, I thought everything belonged to him.'

'I knew the shop belonged to Adam, but I'm sure Grandfather bought things for himself from time to time.'

'Wouldn't that have made the record-keeping difficult?'

'No, he kept his own transactions separate, and his private library was kept at his flat.'

The *patron*, who had been hovering near the table, offered dessert. Drew refused brusquely, but ordered brandies.

★ ★ ★

When they arrived, Francesca said doubtfully, 'Could Mr. Pinkerton have

151

afforded to buy such books for himself? We're talking about something like thirty thousand pounds.'

'I know it sounds unlikely, but I'm sure Cochran agrees that the atlases belonged to my grandfather, although I can't quite pin him down. I think Adam has been influencing him.'

'Drew, that's ridiculous. If the atlases are yours, you'll get them. The ownership of such valuable things can certainly be proved. I don't see eye to eye with Adam over a lot of things, but in business matters he has a reputation for complete integrity.'

'Well, I hope you're right,' Drew said rather sulkily. 'You can't remember anything Adam said about them that might give us a clue?'

Francesca thought hard. She was tired after her long, eventful day, and the wine and brandy did nothing to sharpen her memory. 'He did say, 'He — your Grandfather, that is — bought them on my advice'.'

'That sounds as though Grandfather

bought them for himself, don't you think?' Drew demanded eagerly.

'Not necessarily. Mr. Pinkerton had used that expression himself, in the past, over books he was buying for the shop. Surely there are records that would clear the matter up?'

'There probably are, but I've no idea where they would be kept.'

Incautiously she said, 'They're on their way here with the books that are coming over.'

'Are you sure?'

'Adam said the books were coming, 'together with all my uncle's records'.'

'Could you have a look at them, do you think, to see if the atlases are mentioned?'

'Drew, I couldn't possibly snoop through Adam's private papers!'

'But I only want what's mine.' He was sounding querulous now. 'Cochran more or less agreed they were mine when I put him on the spot — phone him if you don't believe me.'

Francesca shook her head unhappily.

There was no doubt that Drew genuinely believed his own claim, and Mr. Cochran was undoubtedly the soul of probity.

'But why?' she said. 'Why would Adam do such a thing? He's a wealthy man.'

'Why?' Drew repeated shortly. 'In order to keep an expensive mistress, that's why.'

The food, the wine, and her tiredness, combined to set her stomach churning. She said, 'Do you mean Gabrielle?'

'Who else? It's always been Gabrielle with Adam, hasn't it?'

'I don't know!' To her dismay, tears of chagrin welled in her eyes. 'How could I know? I've only just come on the scene.'

'But haven't you see anything of Gabrielle? She's usually around.'

She drew a steadying breath. 'Yes, I've seen her. In fact, I've been to dinner at her house.'

'Didn't you realise that she and Adam were lovers?'

'I rather assumed they were. I'd seen

— seen the way they behaved together. I'd seen, I don't know how many photographs of Adam escorting her. But — for heaven's sake, Drew — her husband is a cripple! Adam spoke of him as one of his oldest friends. How could he be so low?'

'Well, I assure you, it's true. They were lovers when I first stayed with Adam in Paris, five years ago.' He broke off and regarded her more closely. 'Fran, are you crying? Whatever's the matter?'

She scrubbed furiously at her eyes. 'I'm afraid I've made something of a fool of myself — '

He stared. 'You don't mean with Adam?'

'Oh, nothing's happened. But I suppose I've been a little infatuated.'

He shook his head. 'Not much hope there, I would think. I mean, you're a great girl — and attractive, too — but Adam's a bit of a sophisticate and beside Gabrielle — well, you've got to admit she's something special.'

⋆　⋆　⋆

Francesca found it depressingly easy to admit.

'But a very expensive lady.' Drew had returned to his obsession. 'Adam may seem wealthy to us, but, compared with de Montbel, he's very moderately fixed. So it might be a temptation for him quietly to appropriate my atlases. We know how ruthless he can be. Surely you haven't forgotten his treatment of my grandfather?'

That was just the trouble, Francesca thought. More and more often she did forget.

'What about it?' Drew pressed. 'What harm could it do, just to look?'

'No,' she said firmly. 'I won't do anything underhand. But if I can think up some pretext for going through the accounts with Adam — to check that I dealt with something correctly, perhaps — I'll do it.'

With that he had to be content. The evening, stripped of any social or romantic pretence, limped lamely to an end, and Drew hailed a taxi for Francesca and despatched her to Montmartre, promising to phone her within a day or two.

To report any development to him, she thought ruefully, as she leant back against the taxi upholstery. She was under no illusions that Drew's sudden increase in interest in her stemmed from anything but the fact that she might be useful to him.

So she had promised to keep her eyes open. It was, in fact, just the sort of situation she had in mind when she first travelled to Paris. The possibility of some way of damaging Adam.

So why wasn't she feeling the slightest spark of pleasure at the prospect? If she was honest with herself, it was because having her suspicions of Adam and Gabrielle's relationship confirmed meant more to her than revenge, or righting an injustice.

As she had told Drew, once she had seen Gaston de Montbel's condition, she had assumed — against all the evidence — that they could not possibly be lovers. The realisation that the obvious had been true all along had hit her a sickening blow.

It was hard to believe that one man could behave so basely to another as Adam had to Gaston — a friend as well as a cripple. Oh, he would, no doubt, attempt to justify his behaviour with sophisticated arguments about having a mistress being 'a practical arrangement', but, as far as she was concerned, a man who could behave in such a way was a rat capable of anything.

The following day turned out to be uneventful. Marcel Vachette started her on overhauling the catalogue, and the careful checking of references suited her mood well.

She saw Adam in passing, once or twice, and he was coolly polite and no more. She arrived home at six-thirty, went out to a nearby café for a quick meal and, on returning to Madame Bauchet's, played chess with Monsieur Karnaukhov.

A thoroughly boring day, Francesca reflected as she pulled the covers over her. Not at all how Paris got her reputation. But after the upheavals of the previous three days it was very welcome. She just wasn't made for that kind of action.

★　★　★

The following day was notable on two counts. A visit to the shop from Sylvie Fournier, and the arrival of the books from Lynford.

Sylvie dropped in out of the blue, at about ten o'clock. She was wearing a mustard-coloured cloak to which the tails of several small furry animals were attached, and, when Francesca saw her, she was swooping round the shop like some exotic bird, plucking books from the shelves at random and dusting her hands off ostentatiously.

Francesca had collected Sylvie's jodhpurs from the cleaners that morning and had been wondering how to return them to her. She fetched the box from the staffroom and ran downstairs.

'*Tiens!*' Sylvie exclaimed when she saw her, 'How do you stand this place? It is very boring, no?'

'No. At least not to me.' Francesca smiled shyly. 'I love it. Here are the jodhpurs I borrowed, Madame Fournier. I've had them cleaned. Thank you for lending me the outfit. It was beautiful, and it was very kind of you to lend it. I'm sorry it got messy.'

Sylvie's expressive mouth turned down. 'It was nothing. But the weather — *quel horreur!* But perhaps the English bloom in such rain, where I would be — what do you say — the drowned mouse?'

Laughing, Francesca had to admit that she, too, had been an exceedingly drowned mouse.

Adam suddenly appeared on the stairs behind them.

'Adam,' Sylvie called. 'I came to take Francesca out to coffee, away from your boring old shop.'

'OK. But don't keep her away more than half-an-hour, and don't lead her astray.'

He was smiling slightly as Francesca, protesting mildly, allowed herself to be shepherded along by Sylvie to a very expensive restaurant in a tiny square not far from the bookshop.

'So,' Sylvie said, when they were settled at a table after a highly dramatic entrance during which the cloak had put a considerable amount of china at risk. 'It was not a great success — the riding?'

'I was enjoying it tremendously until the storm, but after that — well, it was a bit of a wash-out!'

'But with Adam — nothing?'

'What do you mean?' But Sylvie's meaning was so obvious that it seemed stupid to hedge. 'Oh, Sylvie, he's my boss, that's all.'

'But you do like him? What woman could not like Adam — so rich and so handsome.'

Smiling at the order in which Sylvie

listed his inducements, Francesca said, 'Of course, I can see that he is very attractive.'

'And you can feel it, too, I know. I could see that on Sunday night. You have not the cool heart that you pretend. So I endeavoured to arrange the tryst. But I did not think there was much hope there. It is too long-established, that *affaire*, and yet it is not good for either of them.'

At a loss for comment, Francesca ventured, 'I liked Monsieur de Montbel very much.'

'Ah, Gaston is a wonderful person. *C'est tragique.*' Sylvie heaved a deep sigh, but it was not in her nature to be despondent for long. 'Content yourself, *chérie*,' she assured Francesca. 'We shall soon find you a companion *très charmant*.'

They finished their delicious hot chocolate, while Sylvie continued to entertain Francesca with anecdotes of her social life. Then, when the stipulated half hour was up, she left her at the door of the Silver Lute, kissing her warmly on both cheeks and promising to telephone.

The books from Lynford arrived after lunch, and Adam asked Francesca to help Vachette to clear some space in the stockroom for them.

She found Marcel Vachette in the larger of the two storerooms, and together they sorted and restacked books until they had made a reasonable amount of space. Then she helped to unpack the books from Lynford and she shared with her colleagues memories of when and where they had been bought, glad that Adam was not around to witness her sentimentality. He had retired to his office with the separately crated, most valuable books, and two large boxes of records and correspondence.

*   *   *

It was six o'clock before they finished cataloguing the books and arranging them on the shelves. Nicole and Celestine had already left for home, and Francesca was about to leave with Monsieur Vachette, when Adam came out of his office.

'Marcel, will you come up for a minute? You too, Francesca. I think you'll be interested.'

Francesca followed Vachette up the stairs to Adam's office, wondering why they had been summoned. In the doorway, frozen like a hunting dog that scents prey, Vachette was staring at two large, leather-bound volumes on Adam's desk. He approached the desk, his eyes still glued to the books. 'Is that the Juan Martinez that went to Frankfurt in February?' he asked in awed tones.

'Yes. The 1585.' Adam gently raised the cover of the second book to reveal the title page. 'And a Braun and Hogenberg *Civitatus Arbis Terrarum*, early seventeenth century.'

'Monsieur Pinkerton bought them?' Vachette asked, with what sounded like surprise in his voice. Then, in his excitement, his English left him, and he broke into a torrent of French as he examined the atlases with reverent hands. Adam answered him in French as he displayed various of the plates in the atlases, and Francesca caught the sums twenty thousand and eighteen thousand pounds. If these were the two books Drew was concerned about — and they almost certainly were — that was a far larger sum than she would have expected Mr. Pinkerton to have available. On the other hand, Marcel Vachette seemed to have known nothing of the purchase, and he was usually involved in additions to stock, particularly such valuable ones.

She became aware that Adam was watching her reaction closely. 'Well, Francesca?' he asked. 'You're very silent. What do you think of them?'

She came closer to the desk and looked down at the Juan Martinez, a portolan atlas, or pilot's book.

The workmanship took her breath away. The careful cartography of coastline and harbour, channels and reefs, were a practical guide to navigation, but out in the ocean and in the 'void places' of the interior, imagination had run riot in brightly-hued vignettes of ships and sea monsters, and fabulous beasts of myth and legend.

She said, 'It's beautiful. It has a sort of — confident innocence.'

'I see what you mean. That was probably because nobody was in the position to prove them wrong.'

She continued to admire the maps, even the compass-roses, scales and dividers — mere working devices — the artist's imagination had tricked out with decorative detail.

'Is the colouring contemporary?' she asked.

'Good heavens, yes! The Antiquarian Booksellers' Association doesn't look kindly on addition by a later hand, or any other form of bastardisation for that matter. There are several partial, or imperfect ones floating about, but a specimen like this is rarer than diamonds.'

He turned back to Vachette and, while Francesca continued to examine the books, she strove to follow their conversation. The manager appeared to be suggesting possible buyers for the new acquisitions, while Adam sounded evasive. Finally he said, 'We'll enjoy them for a little while ourselves, before we decide anything.'

He put the books away in the safe, and Vachette hurried off to the métro. Unwilling to be left alone with Adam, Francesca hastened after him, but was recalled once more.

'Francesca. I'm sorry, I should have given this to you earlier.'

Reluctantly she retraced her footsteps to the office. Adam stood by the open safe, a thick envelope in his hand.

Francesca took it from him. 'What is it?'

'Cochran included it with the rest of the stuff, but it's for you. A bequest from my uncle, apparently.'

★   ★   ★

'Oh!' With eager fingers, she tore open the envelope to reveal a small book bound in dove-grey vellum. She looked at it and tears started to form in her eyes. She blinked hard. 'It's the Oriel Press edition of Shakespeare's *Sonnets*,' she said, her voice sounding rough. 'He knew how much I loved it.'

Adam took the book from her and flicked through the pages, then stopped. '*Shall I compare thee to a summer's day? Thou art more lovely and more temperate*,' he read, in a deep, warm voice that sent shivers down her spine. He looked up and their eyes met for a moment, then he returned to the book, noting its elegant type and creamy handmade paper.

'Very nice,' he said. 'The Oriel was one of the best private presses of the 'Twenties. All their work was of a high standard.' He handed the book back to her. 'It would fetch something like a hundred pounds.'

'I'd starve before I'd part with it!' she snapped. She restored the book to its wrapping, slipped it into her handbag, and ran downstairs and out of the shop.

One thing could be said for Adam Preston, she thought. As soon as she began to weaken a little in her contempt for him, he could be relied on to do, or say, something completely insufferable.

When she reached the Boulevard Saint Michel, she decided, on the spur of the moment, to pay a call on Drew. He had told her where he lived and it was not far off. She pushed her way through the usual milling crowds on the boulevard, and turned off into the ancient thoroughfares behind the Sorbonne. She soon located Drew's lodging, a surprisingly shabby edifice. A trio of grubby, but beautiful, Arab children were playing on the step and they watched Francesca with huge, dark eyes as she approached the narrow hallway.

Once inside, from behind closed doors, a medley of cooking smells assailed her nose, and a riot of many tongues assaulted her ears. She stood and looked around her helplessly. After a minute, the largest of the children approached her and said something in an incomprehensible dialect. Francesca smiled, shaking her head, but the boy took her hand in his grimy paw. '*Le blond Americain*,' he said, trying to draw her towards the back of the house.

The blond American. To an Arab child that might describe Drew. She nodded, and the boy indicated a door across a tiny courtyard.

She went through the open back door and crossed the cobbled yard that was furnished with washing-lines and a few tired-looking plants. A score of dirty windows looked down into it, and the smell was sour and unpleasant.

She tapped hesitantly at the door the boy had indicated and, a moment later, it opened somewhat cautiously, and Drew looked out.

'Francesca!' he exclaimed in amazement. 'What on earth are you doing here?'

She smiled. 'I just happened to be in the neighbourhood. No, seriously, Drew, the Lynford books arrived today and the two atlases were among them. At least, I assume they were the same two.'

'Here?' He was instantly alert. 'Come inside. No, don't come in. I'll get my jacket, there's a decent bar on the corner.'

★ ★ ★

He took her firmly by the arm and propelled her along the narrow passage of the street. At a pleasant bar on the corner of the street, they settled down with a carafe of wine.

'Why should Cochran have sent the atlases here?' Drew asked. 'I don't understand it.'

'Because they belong here, I imagine,' Francesca said. 'Drew, together they cost thirty-eight thousand pounds. Surely Mr. Pinkerton couldn't afford to spend that sort of money?'

Drew gasped. 'Thirty-eight thousand? Are you sure?'

'Quite sure. Adam was discussing

them with Monsieur Vachette.'

'Did he say anything else about them?'

'He talked about the workmanship, the colouring methods — '

'No, no,' Drew interrupted impatiently. 'I mean, what he intends to do with them.'

'Monsieur Vachette suggested possible clients who might be interested in them. They would have to be very wealthy, of course.'

'But he can't sell them!' Drew broke in furiously. 'What did Adam say?'

'He was evasive. I don't think he intends to sell them for a while.'

'I should damn well think not!' He seemed to be aware of a hesitancy in her. 'Was there something else?'

'It was just that Monsieur Vachette didn't seem to have known anything about the atlases previously. About their purchase, I mean. It seemed to be a complete surprise to him.'

'Would you normally expect him to?'

'Yes. He's usually closely involved in what's bought. Adam discusses things with him. I know he occasionally marks things in sale catalogues that Adam might have missed. With such important items — and even at the Lute the atlases are pretty special — it's hard to understand why they had never been mentioned. Monsieur Vachette said — ' she faltered.

'Yes?' Drew pressed.

'He said, 'Mr. Pinkerton bought them?' And he sounded amazed.'

Drew leant back in his chair and regarded her soberly. 'That's it then. Grandfather didn't buy them as Adam's agent, he bought them for himself.'

'Oh, Drew, it might not mean anything. I don't suppose Adam tells Monsieur Vachette everything, especially about the Lynford end of things. Think of the sum involved, thirty-eight thousand pounds. Mr. Pinkerton didn't have that kind of money.'

'How do you know? Were you privy to his bank account?' he snapped peevishly. He recovered himself at once. 'Sorry, Fran. I'm a bit uptight about this business. I hear a lot about Adam's famous business integrity, but what's to prevent him just hanging on to the atlases and doing me out of everything?'

'Mr. Cochran, for one thing.'

'Adam could be cutting him in.'

'Drew, this really is nonsense. You only have to see Cochran!'

'Have you ever seen a picture of Dr. Crippen? A more respectable-looking individual you'd never meet.' He drained his glass. 'Let's go and get something to eat.'

They returned to the boulevard and found a bright impersonal self-service bar where they collected a grill. When they got back to their table, Drew said, 'What about the records from Lynford?'

Francesca had been hoping the whole conversation was over. 'They came with the books,' she said reluctantly.

'Are they in the safe?'

'They were on Adam's desk when I left.'

'Have you got a key to the shop?'

She stared in horror. 'No, I haven't.

And if I had, I wouldn't use it to sneak in.'

Drew toyed with his food sulkily. 'Really, Fran, I can't understand you. I thought you would want to help. When you left Lynford, hanging would have been too good for Adam. But now that you're hot for him — '

The crude expression sickened Francesca, not least because of the grain of truth in it. Suddenly the food tasted like sawdust and she pushed it aside. 'In any case, Adam was still on the premises when I left,' she mumbled.

Once again, their evening ended on a sour note. They drank a glass of wine, while Drew worked desperately to restore their relationship. As they walked down the boulevard to the métro station, he flung an arm across Francesca's shoulders, but it felt like a millstone to her. At the station entrance, he said, 'Will you be all right alone?'

'Yes, of course. It's only nine o'clock.'

He hesitated. 'Francesca, please forgive me. It was a foul thing to say.'

'Drew, if I could believe what you claim is true — and I know you believe it — I would do anything in my power to help.'

'That's my girl.' He pulled her gently towards him and, because for a moment he was the old Drew from Lynford days, and he was all that she had, Francesca clung to him. And, as she did so, she noticed over his shoulder Adam's car slip out into the stream of traffic and his face, darkly questioning, turn towards them.

5

Francesca pushed Drew away from her. 'Drew, that was Adam's car! He just turned up the Boul'Mich.'

Drew stared up the boulevard, but already the car was lost to sight. 'He must have turned into Saint Germain, that's where he has his flat. What a pity you haven't got a key to the office — now that we know the coast is clear.'

Her expression hardened. 'Please don't start that again. I'll keep my eyes and ears open, but I won't do anything more.'

Drew walked her down the platform and, a second later, her train rattled in.

Back in her room Francesca tried to read a book in the hour before bed, but it was impossible to concentrate and, in the end, she put it aside and sat at her window, looking out over the city as she often did at night.

The confusion over the ownership of the atlases was an unpleasant new complication. It was no business of hers, but she seemed to have been drawn into it. She sighed heavily and prepared for bed, hoping that, one way or another, the dispute would quickly be settled.

The following morning she left the house and journeyed across Paris to work. She reached the shop at nine-thirty to find that Nicole was absent with *la migraine*.

'I'm sorry to be late,' Francesca said, relieving Celestine at the mail desk with Marcel Vachette.

'Mr. Preston has had to go to Neuilly. A private house sale that may have some good things,' Vachette told her as they sorted the pile of mail into what they could deal with, and what would require Adam's attention. 'A nuisance it is today, because the books from Lynford make much work. If we have time later, we finish cataloguing them and you can sort the papers that came with them.'

Francesca could scarcely believe this gift from the gods. 'Did Mr. Preston say I was to go through the papers?'

Vachette looked at her, briefly curious. 'No, he don't say, but who knows better than you about Monsieur Pinkerton's records? You help him with them, no?'

Francesca agreed that she had. She picked up the pile of letters requiring only a formal reply. There seemed to be far more than usual, but she raced through them as fast as she could and hurried back to Vachette.

The manager was lost in admiration. 'So neat — and so fast! Now you type out the catalogue slips just so good.'

Her heart sank as she took the thick wad of slips. It looked as though her chance of an unsupervised pry through the Lynford papers was fading. But she beat all her own records to finish the typing and was back to Vachette with the completed work just before noon.

Once again he was full of praise. 'Do

you want to go to lunch now?' he asked. 'You do not take your coffee break.'

'I'd prefer to go later. I was a bit late coming in. I thought I might have a preliminary look through the Lynford papers.'

'Just as you like. Me, I am ready for my lunch.'

They went into Adam's office. 'I expect you can find your way in them,' Vachette said, indicating the boxes. 'Perhaps we find some more surprises, yes? Ah, those atlases — *merveilleux!*'

'You knew nothing about them?' Francesca enquired casually.

'Nothing. Who would imagine *le vieux* Pinkerton would acquire such things.'

'But Mr. Preston would have known?' she probed cautiously.

'Oh, yes, he would know. Monsieur Pinkerton would not spend so much money without his go-ahead.'

'Odd that he didn't mention them to you.'

'Perhaps he thinks to surprise me,'

Vachette replied, but Francesca thought a faint shadow of doubt passed over his face.

As the manager prepared to leave, she said, 'When do you expect Mr. Preston back?'

'He intended to lunch at Neuilly, so probably not until around three o'clock.'

★ ★ ★

He left the office and Francesca heard his small feet tapping down the stairs. She peeped over the staircase and saw Celestine involved with a group of customers and knew that nothing would induce her to leave her post. Slipping back to Adam's office, she closed the door and seated herself at his desk, the two boxes of records in front of her.

Her first emotion was a catch in her throat at the familiarity of the documents — the letters, invoices, bills and catalogues that she typed and filed a hundred times in the little shop at

Lynford. She could almost hear Oswald Pinkerton's gentle voice as he chatted to her.

Then she hastily pushed sentiment aside and got down to work. In an hour, Monsieur Vachette would return and expect her to take her lunch break, or, worse, Adam might return unexpectedly early. But, at least, she could tell him that Vachette had given her permission to handle the papers.

She had organised Mr. Pinkerton into keeping his previously chaotic records tidily, and disposing of them when they were no longer required, and most of the documents in the boxes fell into obvious categories. In half-an-hour, Francesca had sorted them into piles, leaving only a few that she didn't feel competent to deal with. There was no mention, anywhere, of the two atlases.

When she had finished, she went to help Celestine in the shop, and, when Marcel Vachette returned, the two women went out for their lunch.

Just before three o'clock Adam returned from Neuilly. Francesca held her breath as he disappeared inside his office. Within a minute he reappeared and yelled irascibly for Vachette.

Francesca said, 'He's with a customer.'

'Oh.' He looked down at her, frowning darkly. 'Do you know who has been rummaging through these Lynford papers?'

'No one has been *rummaging* through them. I was sorting them out.'

His frown deepened. 'I realise that you like to make yourself indispensable, Francesca, but the Silver Lute has managed to function for a good many years without you to organise us.'

She flushed. 'I'm sorry. I've handled those same papers so many times in the past, I didn't realise there was anything secret about them. In any case, Monsieur Vachette asked me to go through them.'

'Well, as you find them so interesting, perhaps you'll stay behind tonight and put me in the picture.'

She nodded her head dumbly. The

thought of being alone with him filled her stupid wayward heart with the usual mixture of guilty excitement and dread, and she had a strong suspicion that he was aware of it.

She managed to put the coming encounter out of her mind for the next three hours, during which she was kept busy in the shop. But when, at six o'clock, first Celestine, and then Marcel Vachette, left for home, and the doors were shut, she spent as long as she possibly could tidying up and straightening the shelves, before reluctantly making her way to Adam's office.

She felt hot and sweaty, although it was a cool evening, and she wiped her palms on her skirt before tapping on Adam's door. It took two raps before he heard her and, when she entered, he looked as though he had forgotten why she was there.

'Oh, yes, the Lynford records. Thank you for staying.'

His desk was clear of everything except the Lynford documents. He switched on his desk-lamp and, in its intimate pool of light, he drew up two chairs so they were placed close together at the desk.

Francesca sat down on one of the chairs, humping it a few inches farther from his as she did so.

He smiled the mocking smile that seemed to turn her bones to water and sat down beside her. 'Now — elucidate,' he commanded.

* * *

At the electric effect of his nearness, Francesca began to tremble helplessly and her voice died in her throat. Leaning as far away from him as she could get, she began to pull the papers, sorted into rubber bands, from the boxes.

'These are customer lists,' she began, but her voice emerged as a husky squeak, and she cleared her throat. 'These are search lists, arranged under author and title of the book wanted, and where Mr. Pinkerton had tried to obtain it. These are bills, both to and from the business — I settled them whenever possible. These are invoices.' As she continued to explain the different categories her voice steadied, although she was aware she was gathering speed as she approached the end of her task.

'Just a minute, slow down!' His strong brown hand closed over hers and the papers she was holding, and she jumped convulsively under his touch. 'You seem very eager to be off. Now, what did you say these were?'

She explained again and his hand slowly released hers. She kept both her hands beneath the table and finished her exposition by nods of the head.

At the end, only the few documents she had been unable to deal with remained.

'Which did you say those were?' Adam asked.

'Those — there.' Francesca nodded furiously.

'I'm sorry — which?' His dark violet eyes were laughing at her.

'Those!' She shot a finger out to touch the pile, before returning it to the security of her lap. At the same moment there came a sudden loud rattle of rain, like machine-gun fire, at the window. She whirled round towards it, her eyes enormous.

'What's the matter now?' Adam enquired. 'You seem in a highly nervous state tonight, Francesca.'

'I'm not in the least nervous. The rain startled me, that's all.'

'It sounds heavy. Maybe we should shelter together again.' His face, so close to hers, was warmly sensual, and she knew he was remembering the earlier rainstorm that had driven them into each other's arms.

'No!' She jumped up and pushed back her chair. 'I mean — I think I'll go and get the métro if you've finished with me.'

'But you'll get absolutely soaked. Come and have something to eat with me first. I kept you late. Perhaps it will have eased off later.'

'No, thank you.' She edged her way round the desk to the door. 'I — I have to get home.' She scurried to the staffroom to fetch her jacket and bag.

When she reached the front door, she found Adam leaning against it, his raincoat slung around his shoulders.

'Are you leaving now?' Francesca asked foolishly.

'The car's outside. I'll give you a lift.'

Francesca started to protest, but Adam unlocked the door to let them out. In the doorway he pulled her to him, so that the raincoat completely covered her, and they ran awkwardly for the car. He bundled her inside and got behind the wheel, shaking the glistening raindrops from his dark head.

He started the car, turned two or three corners, and stopped again. They were not in the Place St. Michel.

'This isn't the métro,' Francesca stated obviously.

'No, this is a restaurant. A thoroughly

respectable restaurant for business meetings,' he added hastily, seeing her dubious expression, 'not romantic assignations.'

And, in fact, the protest in her was dying away. The contrast between returning, in pouring rain, to a chilly room and a meagre supper, and dining with Adam in the restaurant at which they had stopped — its golden lamps glowing warmly through the windows and its delectable smells creeping out to the car — was simply too great.

'Well, just until the rain stops,' she said ungraciously.

They dashed from the car to the luxurious comfort of the restaurant.

★　★　★

The wine quickly arrived and, as she sipped, she began to relax a little. As she looked around the room she rather doubted the 'business' being transacted at some of the discreetly lit tables, but she determined to keep their own encounter on a strictly unemotional level.

It didn't help that Adam's eyes were appraising her so frankly across the small table.

'I haven't thanked you yet,' he said. 'You had gone through my uncle's papers most efficiently.'

As usual, she wasn't sure she liked his phrasing, but she said, 'Everything was quite straightforward. You should have seen the way things were when I started to work for him — total chaos!'

'But you soon got things organised?'

Francesca said defensively, 'Mr. Pinkerton seemed to appreciate it.'

'I'm sure he did. Believe me, I noticed a great difference here in the communications we received from Lynford.'

Their orders arrived and, for a few minutes, Francesca concentrated on the delicious food. Then she said, 'Did Mr. Pinkerton ever do any dealing on his own behalf?'

She had given considerable thought

to a tactful way of wrapping up the vital question, but somehow it had just slipped out, bluntly unembellished. Adam was so obviously a man who could see through the most skilful smokescreen that guile seemed pointless.

He looked at her guardedly, his glass to his lips. 'Why do you ask?'

She shrugged lightly. 'Oh, I just wondered. Bookselling doesn't seem to be the sort of job one does only as an agent. I would have thought it was irresistible to make purchases for oneself.'

'You're quite right. Of course, my uncle made private purchases. Surely you've seen the books at his flat? He had a very nice collection.'

It wasn't a complete answer to her question and he knew it. After a long pause in which he sipped his wine, still watching her coolly, he said, 'And, yes, he did deal in the market, often — dare I say it to such a high-minded young lady — at a considerable profit.'

'I thought he probably did. And his personal financial transactions were kept separately, I presume?' Again the question, which she had intended to be so subtle, emerged as brutally obvious. 'I mean — I would hate to have got the accounts mixed up,' she finished lamely.

'I know exactly what you mean. But you're too conscientious. It's out of your hands now, you don't need to worry any more. Eat up your dinner, it will get cold.'

She glared at him in exasperation, but could think of no way to continue the inquisition.

For the remainder of the meal he behaved with perfect, even exaggerated, courtesy. It wasn't until coffee had been brought that he suddenly said, 'Don't you think we might stop beating about the bush and bring this out into the open?'

Francesca jumped as though stung, spluttering slightly over her coffee. 'I don't know what you mean,' she said faintly.

'Come off it, Francesca. Your line is the poor but honest working girl and I must admit you're very good at it. Who put you up to this interrogation?'

At a loss for words she twisted miserably at the napkin in her lap.

Adam seemed to take pity on her. 'It was Drew, wasn't it? I seem to discern his hand in this. Don't have any illusions about that sunny charm, Francesca. He's a very ruthless young man. He'll make use of you for his own questionable ends and then he'll jettison you.'

'*His* questionable ends?' Her eyes challenged his. 'Drew only wants what he's entitled to. What's wrong with that?'

'Nothing at all. And Drew has got what he's entitled to — a nice little fortune, without the slightest exertion on his part.'

Some demonic fury drove her on. 'What about the atlases?' she demanded.

* * *

The cold still look in his eyes pulled her up short. In icy tones he said, 'Oh, yes, the atlases. I thought we would be getting to those.'

He said nothing further. With a trembling hand, Francesca restored her coffee cup to her saucer and it rattled loudly. Suddenly positive, she said, 'They belong to Drew. You have no right to them.'

'Let's just say I'm taking care of them for a while.'

She stared at him blankly. 'But they are his!'

'We don't always get what's coming to us in this life, as you should know.' He sipped his brandy calmly. 'The atlases are too good for him.'

His shameless admission of theft took Francesca's breath away. Her mouth opened and shut wordlessly. When she had recovered slightly, she said, 'Why don't you make him an offer for them?'

'Why doesn't your accomplice deal with me directly?'

'My *accomplice*?'

'Oh, I'm sure you have a more acceptable name for him. Lover? No, maybe that's a little strong for such a virtuous young woman. Boy friend, perhaps — or sweetheart?'

Even through her own agitation, Francesca could see that Adam was losing his usual self-possession. His voice was raised and his hands trembled against the table edge.

Trying to defuse the situation, she said, 'I admit Drew discussed the atlases with me. He was confused and worried about their ownership. But — although I fail to see that it's any of your business — he is simply a friend, nothing more.'

'As my uncle was a friend?'

'Not in the same way. I loved Mr. Pinkerton — '

'Ha!' Adam gave a triumphant snort that caused the diners at adjacent tables to turn and look at them.

'It wasn't like that!' Tears of frustration that had been welling in her eyes spilled over on to her cheeks. She struggled to push her chair back in the confined space. 'There's simply no point in talking to you. You turn everything I say against me. I'm leaving!'

His hand shot out, imprisoning her wrist with a brutal strength. 'No, you're not. Your first instinct is always to take flight. What's the good of running away? I meant what I said about bringing everything out in the open. Don't you think we might try to be honest with each other? I'll try to understand.'

Francesca stared at him through her tears. Both the ice and the fire had left his eyes, to be replaced by an expression that dumbfounded her — a mixture of pain and longing.

In his moment of weakness she adroitly twisted her wrist from his grasp. '*You'll* try to understand? Am I supposed to confess to something? I'm sorry, but I feel completely innocent. *I'm* not a thief — and I wouldn't make love to a crippled friend's partner!'

The moment the words were out of her mouth, she was horrified. Adam had stepped back and was looking at her with revulsion. In the hiatus, she slipped past him and pushed her way between the tables of fascinated diners, to the door.

She had forgotten the rain which fell in a solid mass, bouncing up ankle-high from the pavement. She had forgotten her jacket and there was no way she was going to make a return appearance in the restaurant to collect it. She had forgotten that she had no idea where she was.

But at least she had grabbed her bag and had money for her métro fare when she could find one. She could not be far from the Boulevard St. Michel — they had only been three or four minutes in the car — in fact, she thought she could hear the hum of its traffic over to her left.

She scurried off in that direction through the curtaining rain. The area was badly lit, and she knew, despite the occasional expensive restaurant, that it wasn't one in which to linger alone at night. Above all else, she longed to get away from Adam Preston — that self-righteous prig. There could be no formality like working out her notice — she never wanted to see him again, and, after what she had just said to him, she was sure he would feel the same about her.

★ ★ ★

She was soaked to the skin within seconds of leaving the restaurant. The rain was so blinding that it was almost impossible to see the way ahead, and she darted into a doorway to get her bearings. At once the sickening smell of stale wine assailed her, and a shapeless mass of rags, slumped in a corner, stirred and grunted an oath.

With a shriek, she fled from the doorway and hared up the street. Reason told her it was only a harmless old *clochard*, but reason had fled. The medieval streets, which she had found so fascinating in the daytime, looked sinister now, the tall houses huddled together, black and secretive, and the labyrinth of narrow alleys seemed to harbour terrifying shapes and shadows.

She paused in her headlong flight. She could no longer hear the hum of traffic, or see the glow in the sky that might lead her to the busy boulevard. The street she was in appeared at first to be deserted, but now she realised there were people lurking in several doorways, singly and in pairs. She could hear the low murmur of their voices and some called out to her, but they did not seem the sort of people from whom it was wise to seek help.

She crossed the road and turned into a rather wider street. She had not been in it for more than ten seconds before she heard the tread of heavy footsteps behind her. She threw a quick glance over her shoulder and could just make out the figure of an enormous man, hunched up against the rain, steadily keeping pace with her.

She quickened her own pace, but not so much that her panic might touch off an urgency in him. With her heart pounding uncontrollably, she realised he was gaining on her.

Panic took over, and she began to run. She ran across the road. There was an alleyway straight in front of her and she dashed into it. She leant against the wall, her breath rasping painfully in her throat, and listened. In the street, the man's footsteps continued on their innocent way.

She drew a shaky breath. She was over-reacting, she told herself firmly. She was letting her imagination run away with her. She must get her bearings and proceed in an orderly manner. She peered around and realised with a flood of relief that she recognised her surroundings. Her messenger duties from the shop had brought her to this street. Just one more turn at the end of it and she would reach the Boul' Mich'.

With a lighter heart she turned in that direction. It was then that she noticed the car cruising slowly along the kerb, its dark bulk infinitely more frightening than the night people from whom she had fled.

She quickened her pace again, but the car stayed just behind her. Impeded by the wet skirt clinging round her legs, she broke into a run again. She had almost reached the corner — she could hear the buzz of humanity from the boulevard — when the car door slammed violently and a man leaped across the pavement to grab her in his arms and pinion her, struggling helplessly, against him.

6

For a moment she fought in terror, as though her life was at stake, then the familiarity of the man's body, and the scent of his expensive cologne, penetrated her blind panic and she attempted to squirm round in his arms.

Adam's face was white with rage. 'You bloody little idiot!' he swore. 'What the hell did you think you were doing? Don't you realise what could happen to you here?' He released her abruptly. 'Get in the car!'

'No! You have no right to order me about. I'm going home by métro.'

'You're not going home. You're coming back to the shop with me.'

'What?' She stared at his face through the teeming rain. Her teeth were chattering, but she pressed on. 'Why should I? I'm never going to the shop again. I'll pay back my salary advance and — and my rail ticket and everything. I'm sick and tired of your insults and insinuations. All you want to do is unload your own feelings of guilt on to me.'

Without warning he grabbed both her shoulders and shook her hard, then stopped abruptly.

For a second he looked appalled at his action. Through gritted teeth he said, 'I'm sorry. I've never hurt a woman before. But *I'm* sick to death of your injured innocent act. Not that it isn't convincing. You're very good — I must remember to congratulate Drew. The angel's face gives you an advantage, of course. But it does begin to pall after a time. And if you say, 'I don't know what you're talking about,' once more, I'll go berserk.'

He took her arm, dragged her to the car, and half-threw her into the front seat.

Past knowing, or caring, what was happening, she crouched against the door, as far away from him as she could get, shivering and streaming water. With a face like thunder, he stamped on the accelerator.

The car drew up outside the shop. Adam pulled her from the car, unlocked the shop door and pushed her inside. Glancing at his scowling face, Francesca wondered if he could be unbalanced. If, indeed, she was any safer here than she had been outside in the streets. He took the stairs two at a time, and wrenched open his office door. Reluctantly she trailed up the stairs behind him.

At the sight of her standing apprehensively in the doorway, huge-eyed, shaking, and soaked to the skin, he pushed past her to the cloakroom and returned with a towel that he threw in her direction.

'Dry yourself!' he commanded.

Without taking her eyes from him, Francesca towelled her face, arms and hair, then, slipping off her shoes, she dried her feet and legs. There was nothing she could do about her soaking dress and she continued to shake convulsively.

She thought his face softened momentarily, but it was gone in an instant as he crossed to the safe and flung it wide.

Automatically she said, 'It wasn't locked?'

'There was no need to lock it,' Adam said bitterly. 'Everything inside is worthless.'

Francesca took a step nearer the safe. There were books piled inside, which looked as if they might be valuable. Bewildered, she looked questioningly at him.

'I took away the atlases, and everything else of value, last night. I thought it advisable — now that you have access to my office.'

★ ★ ★

For a moment she did not register what he had said. Then the colour slowly drained from her face and she stared at him, her smudgy eyes enormous against the pallor.

'I'm not a thief,' she whispered. Then

outrage rallied her spirits. 'You're doing it again! *You* are the thief! You admitted it.'

'I didn't say you were a thief. I only wish you were!' Adam was pulling the books from the safe and tossing them roughly on to the desk. 'Look here! And here!'

He was opening the books at places where they had been marked by slips of paper. 'Do you still claim to know nothing of this?'

Francesca drew nearer, uncomprehending. She could see nothing wrong.

'Oh, it's been cleverly done.' His tone was icy. 'You were deceiving experts. The pages of a book of this age are often unnumbered, and the list of plates is sometimes not easy to find, but it's been gutted. Plates have been removed.'

'What!' Francesca turned her attention frantically from one book to another.

'It's only too true. I've received reports of seventeen books in all — with nearly forty plates missing from them. I don't object in principle to books being split up — if the book is of little intrinsic value and there are plenty of copies of it about. Hordes of booksellers make a profitable sideline out of selling separate plates. But these books are all fairly rare, and their illustrations are an integral part of them. Can't you understand that?'

'Of course I can understand it. I dislike the practice of gutting altogether.' Sick and stunned, Francesca sank on to Adam's chair. The brilliant colours of the remaining plates, exotic birds, flowers and plants, swam and merged before her eyes.

'And there's another angle,' his voice continued inexorably. 'My reputation — which happens to be very important to me. I'm supposed to be something of an authority, dealing with serious collectors, and I'm selling them vandalised rubbish cut up like a child's colouring book. Seventeen books that were sold from Lynford in this condition have come back to me, with threats of legal action, cancellations of long-standing accounts, and abuse that I will leave to your imagination. There may be more to come when they are discovered.'

Francesca gazed up at him in horror. There was no doubt in her mind that what he was saying was true. He had the look of a man who has been terribly wounded. As he returned her gaze, there was such hatred and bitterness in his eyes that she had hoped never in her life to see.

'So you see, my dear Francesca, I really had no choice but to close the Lynford business down. I had lost nearly two thousand pounds — not of the utmost importance to me, although you may find that hard to believe; my reputation was being tarnished, and fine books were being vandalised.'

At last she found her voice. 'It was nothing to do with Mr. Pinkerton,' she whispered.

'I'm quite aware of that. But my uncle obviously wasn't in control of his charming young playmates. His sight had deteriorated, he left any close work to you, he couldn't see what was going on. But, all the same, he was easily fooled. A girl like you, content to work in a small-town bookshop for a tiny salary? Drew paying him some attention for the first time in his life? How did he account for his sudden popularity?

'When I first saw you, I thought you might have been the attraction for Drew, but, with him, there usually has to be money in it as well.'

She shook her head dumbly. 'I didn't know. I didn't know anything about it.'

'You expect me to believe that? You and Drew turned up at the same time. You took things over — '

'I didn't. I just helped out where I could.'

'Oh, God, your self-righteous attitude! That's what sickens me most of all. When I brought you over here, I wanted to try to sort out just what had been going on, how involved you were.

I knew my uncle thought highly of you and I wanted to be fair. I thought perhaps you had acted under Drew's influence. Young as he is, he had been in trouble more than once before. But all I got from you, from the beginning, was condemnation — as though it was I who was responsible for my uncle's death.'

'That's what I thought,' Francesca murmured. In the face of these horrible revelations, it was hard to remember just what had been her convictions. 'Mr. Pinkerton got your letter and he just seemed to shrivel up. He never told me what was in the letter — only that you were closing the shop. Drew said it was because it didn't make enough money. And I overheard Mr. Pinkerton pleading with you on the phone — '

'Not to save his shop. I admit I threatened, in the heat of the moment, to close it down, but if he could have put his house in order, I would have let him carry on. No, I had threatened Drew with criminal charges and my uncle was pleading, successfully, with me to drop them.'

'Here.' Adam opened a drawer of his desk and took out a letter. It looked familiar, and Francesca realised it was the letter that had so much upset Mr. Pinkerton, and started off the whole chain of events. 'It was in the box of documents from Lynford. I took it out before you got at them. Read it.'

★   ★   ★

Francesca opened the letter and read it in silence. Basically, it was an account of events just as Adam had related them to her — that vandalised books were being sold from the Lynford shop and that it was rebounding on him, and that he believed Drew to be responsible. The letter was angry and bitter, but it was not harsh, and, from beyond her misery, she felt a small spark of consolation that her heart had not chosen a callous, dishonourable man, but one who — despite his flaws

— cared deeply for his uncle.

She returned the letter to its envelope. 'I can see now why he was so shattered.'

'That's why I couldn't let Drew get hold of the atlases. Acquiring them was the summit of my uncle's life. How could I let them go to him — to break up and sell around junk shops and flea markets for a tenner a plate?'

He was arched over her, close and terrifying in his anger. But a thought struck Francesca, so devastating in its import, that she had to give voice to it.

She looked up at him, her big dark eyes pleading. 'Adam, your uncle didn't believe I was involved in this, did he? I just couldn't bear that. He trusted me — '

Without warning, he snatched her up from her chair and shook her until her teeth rattled.

'Stop it! You can drop the act now. You and Drew killed that poor old man. You broke his heart!'

This was what had really hurt him

most, Francesca realised. Not the money, or the vandalism, or even his reputation, but the deceiving of a loving, trusting old man.

'No,' she managed to gasp. 'No. I knew nothing about it!' The last reserves of her strength were drained and she drooped, defeated, on to his chest.

His arms moved swiftly round her, pulling her tightly to him, and they clung together for a moment. She felt his body pressing hard against her thin wet dress. With one hand he raised her chin and stared into her face as though his eyes would suck out her soul.

'Oh, Francesca. Do you think I don't want to believe you?' he groaned. He thrust her roughly from him and turned away, raking a hand through his hair.

When he spoke again, he had got his voice under control. 'There is one more point. When I was in London recently, I made some enquiries among the trade. Two booksellers had been offered plates missing from these books. In both cases, the vendors were a young man and woman. Their descriptions of the man closely resembled Drew — and the young woman, you. And if I had any last remaining doubts, your intimacy with Drew since he arrived in Paris would have dispelled them. You'd better collect any belongings you have here. I'll take you home.'

Francesca stood swaying slightly, her face ashen. 'I have nothing here,' she said. 'And I don't want you to take me home.'

He seemed about to protest, but her expression stopped him. She pushed her feet into her wet shoes, walked from the office and down the stairs. She had reached the door of the shop when the silence behind her broke. The office door crashed back and Adam erupted on to the landing.

'Go to your lover!' he yelled after her. 'You can always manage to find your way to him!'

Francesca looked up at him, appalled at the annihilation of his usual suave control. She was about to retort, for what seemed the hundredth time, that Drew was not her lover, but denial seemed pointless. She opened the door and stepped out into the night.

* * *

The rain had stopped and the sky was clear, apart from a handful of tiny clouds scudding across the face of the full moon.

She shivered, but automatically, not really aware of her discomfort. Her legs somehow carried her to her door.

Her teeth chattering, she slipped inside her room. She stripped off all her clothes and put on her dressing-gown. She put a pan of milk on the ring to heat, towelling her hair as she waited. When the milk was hot, she made coffee and sat down with it in front of the small gas-fire.

Everything she had done since she left the office of the Silver Lute had been done without conscious thought, like an automaton. But now, in the quiet of her room, the brutal awareness of her plight flooded in on her. She had no job and very little money. Unless she could find some sort of work immediately, she would have to give notice to Madame Bauchet within a few days. She had no one to turn to. Drew had been her only ally, and it sickened her to think of him.

Although her mind cringed from it, she thought of the shame of exposure — to the staff at the shop, to Sylvie and Gaston, and, most of all, to Gabrielle — when Adam explained her sudden departure. She thought of the cruel injustice of the false accusation, when she would have died rather than hurt Mr. Pinkerton, and forlorn tears ran down her nose and into her coffee cup.

It became impossible to drink any more. The liquid would not pass the lump in her throat. She put her cup down on the floor, rested her head on her arms, and cried as though her heart would break. And as she wept, she acknowledged to herself for the first time that she loved Adam utterly and completely, and all rational thought was swept aside by a flood of longing to be held close, once more, in the haven of his arms.

Some time later, she did not know how long, she had dragged herself to bed, and, at long last, sleep had come.

She woke the following morning feeling headachy and wretched, but determined to take control of her life. She had decided, during the long, sleepless hours, to present her sudden departure from her job as the outcome of a lovers' tiff, to Madame Bauchet. Hopefully this would meet with more sympathy than dismissal. Then she must start the search for another job.

She rose, bathed and dressed, and ventured downstairs in search of her landlady. The result was just as she had hoped. Madame Bauchet was intrigued and sympathetic and — although refusing to accept Francesca's situation as permanent, and convinced that

Adam would soon arrive pleading for her return — she nevertheless produced a couple of newspapers that listed current job vacancies.

As she hunted through them, Francesca's heart sank. There was very little that appealed to her, or for which she was in any way qualified. In some cases she had considerable difficulty even understanding the job requirements. Nonetheless, she spent the next four days diligently tramping the boulevards to attend interviews, only to meet with courteous, but unvarying refusal.

On the evening of the fourth day, she returned exhausted to her room, slipped her shoes from her aching feet and lay down on her bed. Almost without regret, she decided that it was time to pack up and return to England. She had little enthusiasm for staying in Paris any longer.

After a few minutes, she got up and pulled her suitcases from the wardrobe, determined to make a start before she went out for her evening meal.

She had scarcely begun when she heard Madame Bauchet mounting the stairs. With a pricking of tears at her eyelids, she remembered the last time Madame had come up to her room. It had been while she was ransacking her wardrobe for something to wear to accompany Adam to the Montbels.

But, this time, Madame Bauchet was not alone. For a moment, wild irrational hope flared in her, but the second footsteps, although impeded by the plodding landlady, were light and quick as a bird's. She went to the door and opened it. Behind a puffing Madame Bauchet, she saw the lively face of Sylvie Fournier.

'*Bonjour*, Francesca,' Sylvie sang out, as she planted a kiss on Francesca's cheek.

'Now, what is this, *chérie?*' she asked as Madame Bauchet turned to descend the stairs again. 'I go to the shop to visit you and you are disappeared. I cannot

219

believe it. What has happened? Why do you leave Adam so quick? At the first little lovers' tiff, you run away and hide.'

'It wasn't like that,' Francesca put in. 'There was no romance between Adam and me — ' An interruption Sylvie appeared to regard as unworthy of notice.

'You must fight for him,' she persisted. 'As I fight for my Philippe. Adam is worth it, I assure you.'

'What is the matter with you French? Are you living a cliché?' Francesca's hands were balled into fists and her voice rose. 'There is no romance between Adam and myself. How often do I have to say it? I didn't come to Paris looking for romance, I came to do a job.'

There was silence between the two women for a moment. Sylvie regarded Francesca shrewdly. 'But you love him,' she said.

The aggression left Francesca. She slumped down on the bed, struggling to control her tears. 'Oh, yes, I love him,' she said. 'But he doesn't know it, and he isn't going to. And he most certainly doesn't love me. But what I said was true, Sylvie. What happened at the Lute was nothing to do with romance. I don't want to go into details — it's too painful — but it was purely a business matter. It was very kind of you to come, but, really, you can't help. I plan to leave France in a day or two.'

Sylvie continued to look at Francesca, her nimble mind skimming through the possibilities of the 'business matter'. Finally she said, 'Is Drew involved? He is charming, that one, but he is not a good man. It would be foolish to put him before a man like Adam.'

Despite herself, Francesca smiled. Inevitably, Sylvie seemed to have veered round to the romantic angle again. 'Drew is involved, but not in the way you mean. Oh, Sylvie, I have to tell someone. Adam believes — he accuses me of being a thief.'

Sylvie stared at her in almost comic horror. 'A thief? But what is to steal? Those dirty old books?'

'They're very valuable — as you know perfectly well. But, no, not the books themselves, that would have been noticed. Someone — Adam thinks it was Drew, and I suppose it must have been — had been removing plates from books in the Lynford shop and selling them separately. A good eighteenth-century watercolour or engraving will fetch quite a lot of money. More, possibly, than they would make as a whole book.'

'Then why does Adam not cut up his own books?' Sylvie asked practically.

'Because for rare books, in good condition, it's a deplorable practice. It's butchery.'

'But why does Adam think that you have done this? Of Drew, yes, I could believe it. But how could he accuse you?'

'It was a very strong coincidence. Nothing of that sort had happened before I came on the scene. And, just about the same time, Drew started to spend more time at the shop. I didn't realise this was a new thing. Anyway, that's when the vandalism began. Then Adam made enquiries in London and learned that a man answering Drew's description, in company with a girl answering mine, had sold some of the missing plates. What else could he be expected to think?'

'But it is unjust!'

Francesca shrugged. 'But understandable. The most horrible aspect is that this business probably hastened his uncle's death and he holds me responsible for that, too.'

'But, I do not understand. If Adam thinks you do these terrible things, why did he bring you to Paris, to his shop?'

'As far as I can make out it was some sort of trial. Mr. Pinkerton had trusted me and Adam wanted to give me the benefit of the doubt. If it was a trial, I seem to have failed miserably.'

'But you must clear yourself! Adam

seems a stern man, but he is just, and underneath he is *gentil*. Gabrielle has told me much of his kindnesses to his staff. It is hard for him to trust people, especially women — '

* * *

'Why?' Francesca put in, surprised. 'Why should that be? I refuse to believe that he could have trouble with women.'

'No, no. Not in his own *affaires*. It goes deeper than that. He speaks little of it, but Gabrielle has told me that, when he was a boy, his mother left his father for a wealthier man. It broke his father's heart.'

'I didn't know that. It explains a lot.'

'It explains, I think, the long *affaire* with Gabrielle. They understand each other. There is no need to trust.'

At the reminder of Gabrielle, Francesca said, 'I can't go back, Sylvie. I simply can't.'

'Because you love him? He thinks of

you much, I can tell. I know he thinks I make the mischief, and it is true. But I wish only good for him and he is very unhappy.'

'Not because of me,' Francesca said bitterly.

'*Non*? Well, listen, I have the little plan. Philippe has a house at St. Clément, near Senlis, just a tiny place where we make the simple retreat. Will you go there for a few days?'

Francesca stared at her. 'It's very kind of you, Sylvie. But, why?'

'Why? For the *vacance*. It is peaceful and beautiful. It will do you good and you can think about what next to do. There are many books there. If you want, you can do what it is you do to them. Arrange them?'

'Catalogue them?'

'Yes, catalogue them. Philippe wishes long to have them catalogued,' Sylvie added with brisk invention.

'But — Philippe? Won't he mind? I've barely met him.'

'What I desire is what Philippe

desires,' Sylvie asserted complacently. 'And anyhow, what is his, is now also mine — and how the Fourniers hate it! So, will you go? It is wrong that you see nothing of France but Paris.'

Francesca hesitated. She was strongly drawn to Sylvie's offer, not least because it would show Adam, if he ever got to know of it, that, despite his accusations, a comparative stranger had trusted her with her house and possessions. It gave her, too, the breathing space she so badly needed.

'All right, I'll go,' she said. 'And thank you very much. But please, Sylvie — no plotting! I absolutely don't want Adam to know where I am.'

'Absolutely *non*,' Sylvie promised solemnly.

'Thank you. But how do I get there?'

'Georges will drive you. I will despatch him at eleven tomorrow morning. Can you be ready? *Oh, la, la,*' she stilled Francesca's protest. 'It is but thirty kilometres and that lazy one has not enough to do. So — it is settled?

Bon. Now I must go.'

Sylvie said goodbye to Francesca, kissing and hugging her, and hared off at great speed down the stairs, and Francesca gave thanks for having found at least one friend. When Sylvie had left, Francesca went directly to Madame Bauchet and explained the situation, whereat the landlady offered to keep her room for two weeks at half rent.

Relieved, Francesca went upstairs. She selected a few suitable clothes and packed them in her smaller case, ready for the next day, tidying the others away. She still regarded the trip as no more than a postponement of her inevitable departure from Paris, but, at the same time, it was mildly exciting to be taking some positive action and setting off into the unknown.

* * *

She woke early the following morning and spent some time shopping in the market for essential food, convinced that Sylvie would never have thought of anything so mundane. Back in her room, she had just packed bread, cheese and pâté, coffee, soap and matches into a basket, when she heard a car-horn from below, and hurried downstairs with her suitcase.

Madame Bauchet was waiting for her in the hall and embraced her almost tearfully, insisting that if she found St. Clément disagreeable she was to return to Place Pascal on the instant.

Georges was standing beside the car, a large, rather surly, figure in his smart grey livery. He took Francesca's suitcase without a word, and put it on the back seat of the car. After a second's hesitation, Francesca got in the front passenger seat, waved to Madame Bauchet, and they turned out of the square into the Rue Norvins.

On the way, Georges told her that Madame Fournier's house was the gatehouse of the château, and that the village was very small. The Fourniers had lived at the château for about three hundred years, but it had been sold and now belonged to a business corporation. The gatehouse, however, had not been sold.

The village of St. Clément, when they drove through it, was indeed small, no more than a score of cottages down either side of the road, a big barn, and a tiny village store. Francesca was still looking back to see it receding in the distance, when Georges turned between two modest gateposts and on to an unmade-up road. A moment later he had stopped before a small house.

With a slight sense of let-down, she said, 'Is this it? Where is the château?'

'It is out of view here, over the hill beyond those trees. These gates are the back entrance. Any guests at the château will use the main drive and gateway. You will be quite private, mademoiselle.'

Maybe more private than I want, Francesca thought. She got out of the car and looked at the house that was to be her home for the next week or two.

It was stone-built and sturdy, the stone yellowed with lichen, and of the plain, almost classical style that suggested early eighteenth-century. It had been reroofed at some time, but otherwise was unembellished. The small garden was completely overgrown; only a mass of tenacious yellow roses had struggled through and clung around the heavy wooden door and the window shutters.

Georges had fetched her case from the car and joined her at the front door. He produced a pair of keys on a ring and, with one of them, unlocked the front door. The room revealed was dark and damp-smelling. Francesca wondered whether Sylvie had ever actually visited the place.

She thought she detected a glimmer of sympathy on Georges' countenance. He went ahead of her into the house and, with difficulty, unfastened the stiff bolts on the windows and shutters, leaving the windows wide. Then he proceeded to switch on the water and electricity.

Reassured that, at least, she had these services, Francesca looked around. In an instant, the rose-scattered sunlight had transformed the place. She saw that, although dusty, it was basically clean. The room was furnished oddly, in what looked like cast-offs from the château; shabby, once-grand pieces in jewel-coloured velvet and chipped gilt rococo, far too big for the room they now occupied.

The house was all on one floor. A door on the left led to a bedroom, another, opposite the front door, led to a kitchen. Georges opened all the windows and inserted a second key in the back door. He returned to Francesca looking, at the same time, impatient to be off and apologetic at leaving her alone.

'Mademoiselle, I should depart. It is a long drive.'

'Yes, you go, Georges. I'll be perfectly all right, and thank you.'

The chauffeur reached into his tunic pocket and brought out an envelope, which he handed to her. 'Madame

instructed me to give you this, mademoiselle.'

Francesca took the letter. 'Thank
you.' She watched Georges turn the car
and head off down the drive back
towards Paris.

★   ★   ★

She returned slowly to the living-room
and opened the envelope. Inside she
found a two hundred franc note and a
brief letter. '*Dear Francesca,*' she read.
'*It occurs to me that there will be no
food in the house. I wonder, will you
be so kind as to get some essentials in?
I believe there is a shop in the village. I
hope all is there for your comfort.
I regret there is no telephone. When you
have enough of the rural life, phone me
from the village and Georges shall fetch
you back. I embrace you. Sylvie F.*'

Francesca returned the letter to its
envelope, cheered by its affectionate
warmth. Sylvie's delicacy in making it
a personal favour to her to provide

Francesca with food was thoughtful, and the money was welcome. Securing her room with Madame Bauchet had left her with very little capital.

The fact that there was no telephone gave her a momentary sense of isolation. But, in a moment, she shook off her depression — she was hardly expecting to get a lot of calls. Resolutely she started on an exploration of her small domain.

Besides the living-room, the bedroom and the kitchen she had already glimpsed, there was a bathroom leading off the kitchen, and a room that seemed to be used as a study, leading off the bedroom. The bathroom suite looked about fifty years old. In the stone-flagged kitchen, there was a small electric cooker, and the wiring and plumbing, though elderly, appeared to be functional. In short, it was the kind of abode where people are quite prepared to rough it for a holiday.

Francesca located the bedding and spread it out to air, then set to with a duster and broom. When the place looked reasonably clean, she filled an old china jug with yellow roses, placed it on the table and started some coffee on the stove.

She enjoyed her coffee with a scratch lunch of bread and pâté, hung up the few clothes she had brought, and decided on an expedition to the village.

She locked the doors of the little house carefully, slipped the keys into her purse, and turned down the dirt road. The cottage was about one hundred yards from the gateless posts which stood a little back from the road. Francesca passed through them and started along the verge of the road.

It was extraordinarily quiet. Only the birds singing and the distant drone of some farm vehicle disturbed the still air. It had grown very hot now that the sun was directly overhead and Francesca realised she had rather misjudged the distance. She had been walking fairly quickly for half-an-hour before the houses of the village came into view. In all that time not a single car had passed her.

She walked the length of the village seeing only three human beings, an elderly man and woman, and a young woman, all at work in their gardens. They looked at her expressionlessly, not acknowledging her shy half-smile.

At the end of the village street, she reached the small shop. She stocked up with a few commodities and, seeing that the shop was also a bar, bought a glass of cider which she carried to a bench outside in the sun.

She drank her cider slowly, preparatory to the long walk back. She was pleased to note a bus-stop beside the bench and, on the wall, a timetable of buses to Senlis, Chantilly and other nearby towns. If the lonely cottage and slumbering village got too claustrophobic, at least she would be able to have a change of scene.

She walked slowly back home, passed only once by a battered Citroën, and was dismayed to find on her arrival that it was still little after four o'clock.

She selected a copy of Daudet which she found in the study, made a cup of tea and, taking a chair outside, sat reading among the roses for an hour. Afterwards, she decided to explore the grounds of the château and, fetching a sweater, walked up the drive that led uphill towards a wood of thickly clustered trees on the skyline.

★   ★   ★

After a few minutes she reached the top of the rise and stopped to look around her. She could see her cottage, the road skirting the estate, one or two isolated homesteads, and, in the distance, the village of St. Clément backed by the dark mass of the forest of Chantilly.

She was determined to get a look at the ex-Fournier ancestral home, but the wood was more extensive than she had thought, and she decided to cut through it, rather than go round. She started off down one of the narrow tracks and, all at once, the sunny world was dark and silent, except for small rustling noises in the undergrowth. Feeling absurdly nervous, she hurried on, whistling bravely, and, in little more than five minutes, had emerged at the far side. Obviously, the wood was a long but shallow strip.

The château was immediately below her, about two hundred yards away, a small, but beautiful, eighteenth-century house, surrounded by formal gardens and manicured lawns. There were two tennis courts behind the house and four limousines parked in front of it, but no signs of life. After a few minutes, feeling rather Cinderella-like, she stole back into the woods and hurried home to her own humble abode.

Back at the cottage, she took as long as she could over preparing her supper, eating it, and washing up. Then, although it was only nine o'clock, she made up her bed and retired with a book. But she couldn't concentrate on reading and, after a few minutes, she put the book aside and switched off her lamp.

The bed was gloriously comfortable, with a deep, old-fashioned down mattress and big feather pillows. Francesca had risen early, and walked long distances in the country air. She expected to sleep fairly soon, but, as she lay there, thoughts of Adam and the searing memory of that last hideous scene in his office, drove sleep from her. She could still see his face twisted in distaste as he looked at her. At the same time, her early relief that he hadn't been guilty of callousness to Oswald Pinkerton was tempered when she remembered his behaviour towards his friend Gaston. His *affaire* with Gabrielle, in the circumstances, was at least as dishonourable as what she had suspected to be his actions towards his uncle.

But perhaps in the second situation he couldn't help himself, she concluded miserably. Gabrielle was very attractive and Adam had shown himself on two occasions with her to be a man of quickly-roused passion. In any event, his relations with the de Montbels were no business of hers, she told herself, turning over fitfully yet again. He was free to conduct such unsavoury liaisons as he pleased. She had not travelled to Paris to avenge Gaston de Montbel.

But the recollection of her own interludes with him were devastating. The bed was sensuously warm and as she tossed and turned she felt again his hands on her body. Her veins seemed to flow fire and her skin was almost painfully sensitive as the memory of him overwhelmed her.

Francesca moaned, turning over her pillow to find some cooler linen and, at last, she slept.

She awoke the next morning drained and exhausted. She crawled out of bed and had a bath which restored her somewhat. After a quick breakfast, she started to polish the furniture with the energy of a dervish. Later in the day she began work on cataloguing the books, taking as long as possible over a neatly hand-written record, with subject and title cross-references.

The next few days followed a similar pattern. She managed to stretch the cataloguing over four days, after which she was left with only meals, reading and walks to occupy her time. She had paid two further visits to St. Clément, but, apart from these, she hadn't seen a living soul. Both day and night she fought a losing battle against the terrible longing for Adam.

★　★　★

On the morning of the fifth day, she discovered a hoard of ancient gardening tools in a cupboard beneath the kitchen sink and, selecting a stout billhook, and securing her hair in a scarf, she sallied outside to reduce the garden around the cottage to some sort of order.

She worked for an hour, without pause, clearing paths and hacking back the smothering roses, aware that, at the same time, she was trying to exorcise Adam's memory — striking at him for reducing her to such a state, at Gabrielle, who had access to his longed-for embraces, and, most of all, at herself, for allowing herself to be so pathetically undermined.

The sun was directly overhead and it was baking hot when she stopped to draw breath. She was dizzy with exhaustion as she noticed, for the first time, the bloody scratches on her hands and forearms where the savage thorns had ripped her. She pulled the scarf from her head and had just decided to go inside and wash her arms, when she heard a car slowly pass the gateposts. It paused, seemed to hesitate, then backed into view before turning into the drive.

Francesca knelt on the path, oblivious to the stones that dug into her knees. She shaded her eyes against the dazzling sun and a wave of pure joy washed over her. The car was a big, dark Renault. She struggled to her feet, conscious of her flushed face and dishevelled hair, the blood and grass-stains on her clothes and limbs. As she did so, the car stopped in front of the cottage, and Gabrielle, immaculate in the Parisian's idea of country-wear, stepped out.

Francesca stood rooted to the spot, quite unable to think of anything to say. Slowly she lowered the hand which first had shaded her eyes against the sun, and then had hidden the quick tears of disappointment that the car was not Adam's. Gabrielle was staring at her in exaggerated horror.

'*Chérie*, it is terrible that you have to do such work! Surely there is some kind of job to be found in Paris — '

Francesca stumbled, 'It's not a job, it's a holiday — '

'*Mon Dieu!* Never will I understand you English — ' Gabrielle glanced doubtfully at the cottage. 'Is it permitted we go in? The sun — so damaging to the complexion.'

Reflecting that her own was probably beyond redemption, Francesca scurried into the cottage ahead of Gabrielle. The latter, wearing fine tweed culottes topped by a tan silk shirt, a totally unnecessary cashmere sweater draped over her shoulders, prowled around the small living-room like a caged panther, throwing open the doors of the adjoining rooms.

'Amusing,' she announced at last. 'The simple life. Does the little Fournier see herself — like Marie Antoinette at Versailles — playing at being a peasant girl?'

'I don't think Madame Fournier has ever been here,' Francesca said defensively. 'And I think the cottage is delightful.' She paused. 'Did — did Sylvie tell you I was here?' she asked.

'No. I would not give her the satisfaction of asking.' Gabrielle flicked her silk scarf at a chair, decided it was fit to sit on, and subsided elegantly. 'I paid a visit to the good Madame Bauchet. I got her address from Nicole. And she would tell me only that you had left in a chauffeur-driven limousine. Who else in Paris would be sufficiently ostentatious to employ a liveried chauffeur but a *nouveau riche* like Sylvie Fournier? Then

I remembered the Fournier château, and the lodge where Philippe and I played together as children. It seemed a highly likely hiding place.'

'But why?' Francesca queried. 'Why did you want to see me?'

Gabrielle studied her speckless chestnut leather brogues. 'Is there, perhaps, some coffee?' she asked evasively.

'Yes, of course.' Aware that she had been standing before Gabrielle, wringing her hands like a housemaid discovered in some misdemeanour, Francesca leaped for the kitchen, glad of the chance to escape. She put a saucepan on to boil, then hastily sponged her face and hands.

'I must look a dreadful sight,' she called back to Gabrielle in the other room.

'Yes,' Gabrielle drawled.

Francesca waited for more, but that seemed to be it. She combed her hair at the little mirror above the sink, wrinkling her nose as much at her unkempt appearance as at the agony of the tangles in her hair.

When the coffee was ready, she carried it into the living-room on a tray.

'It's only instant, I'm afraid,' she apologised, ready to cringe as the cup approached Gabrielle's exquisite mouth. Then, suddenly, she thought, I'm damned if I'll be intimidated by her rudeness. It's not her house and nobody invited her here. She said bluntly, 'You were going to tell me why you had come.'

Gabrielle took a long drink of her coffee as though it was quite palatable. 'I'm really not sure,' she said at last. 'I suppose I was curious about your sudden disappearance.'

'Is it any of your business?' Francesca asked bravely.

Gabrielle shrugged her slim shoulders. 'Perhaps not, but Adam is a good friend, and your going seems to have had an extraordinary effect on him.'

Francesca lowered her eyes to her cup. 'In what way?'

'In all ways. He doesn't want to go

out in society. He is sullen and bad tempered. No longer is he the charming companion.'

Francesca drew a long breath. 'But, Madame, you cannot imagine his — his mood is anything to do with me?'

'It is incredible, I admit,' Gabrielle said coolly. 'But the timing makes such a conclusion inevitable. I never saw such a change in a man. Frankly he is a bore.'

'Madame de Montbel, there are other reasons,' Francesca began carefully. No way in the world was she going to tell Gabrielle of Adam's suspicions of her. 'I know of them. They do concern Adam and me, but they are not romantic, if that is what you imagine.'

Gabrielle looked at her for a long time, until Francesca squirmed beneath the worldly-wise gaze. Then the other woman selected a cigarette from a slim gold case and lit it from a matching lighter. She shook her head a little doubtfully.

'I have an instinct about these things and I am in no doubt that you have fallen in love with Adam. That was to be expected. But, on his part? You have a certain appeal, it is true, but Adam does not easily allow himself to become involved.'

Francesca stood up. She put down her cup with a hand that trembled slightly. 'I admit that I allowed myself to become infatuated with Adam, and, for my part, that was the reason for my leaving the shop. On his side it was something else entirely. So, you see, Madame, you have nothing to fear from me.'

Gabrielle continued to smoke. Her head was thrown back to study the standing Francesca and the fierce sunlight, penetrating the room, brutally revealed the faint lines about her eyes and mouth.

She said, 'You have relieved my fears. I was beginning to think I must look around for a new companion. Not that I expect to have any difficulty in finding replacements for a few years yet, you understand. In fact, I was almost looking forward to a change. Our relationship has been going on for a long time and these things can get a little stale.'

'Like marriage, Madame?' Francesca put in bitterly.

'Oh, no, not at all like marriage. And you must not confuse the two.'

'Of course. I forgot. Adam has pointed out to me, more than once, that in France, marriage is a practical matter involving property and position.'

Gabrielle looked curiously at the younger woman. 'Not my marriage, I assure you. I fell madly in love with my husband in a fashion even a little romantic like you would approve.'

'But it didn't stop you taking a lover when you began to tire of your husband. A husband who is a — a helpless cripple,' Francesca blurted out.

* * *

There was a deadly silence. Appalled, Francesca wondered if she had gone too far.

In a voice little above a whisper,

Gabrielle said, 'What you must think of me! And what you must think of Adam!'

Francesca sat down again slowly. She said wretchedly, 'I shouldn't have said what I did. It's none of my business. I apologise, Madame.'

Gabrielle hesitated. Then she said, 'Do you know how long Gaston and I have been married, *chérie?*'

Francesca stared. 'No.'

'Less than a year. Ten months, to be exact. Adam and I were lovers for a long time, six or seven years, and it was very good. Then he introduced me to Gaston and we fell head over heels in love. Two months later we were married.'

'And Adam?' Francesca queried.

Gabrielle shrugged slightly. 'He accepted it. What else? To be a mistress is to wait for the right match. But, you must understand, from the day of my engagement to Gaston, he has never touched me.'

Tears of shame filled Francesca's

eyes. 'I see. Oh, Gabrielle, I'm sorry. I thought such vile things.'

'That is quite understandable. It is the way outsiders see our liaison — in a way, it is how I want them to see it. I could not bear to be thought a loser — to have made a bad bargain.'

'A bad bargain? But surely you knew what you were taking on?' Francesca ventured.

'How so? Before Gaston was thrown from his horse on our honeymoon, he was one of the finest amateur sports-men in France. Afterwards, when it looked certain that his injuries would be permanent, he persuaded Adam — much against his will — to resume his old rôle as my escort.'

Francesca covered her face with her hands. In a muffled voice she said, 'I misunderstood everything. I'm so ashamed of myself.'

'It wasn't your fault. As I said, that was the picture I tried to present to the world. Gaston, Adam and I, and our closest friends, knew the true position, and that was all that mattered.' She paused, then gently parted Francesca's hands to reveal her tear-soaked face.

'Maybe our charade was unfair to Adam, although I thought it suited him, too. I was — presentable, familiar, and he doesn't form relationships easily. But if you think there is a chance of an *affaire* between you, I will — how do you say — step out of the picture?'

Francesca's tears began to flow afresh. 'Oh, no, there is no chance of that, believe me, Gabrielle. But, thank you, you are a very nice woman.'

'*Tiens!* Heaven forbid,' Gabrielle exclaimed in horror. 'But it is not chic to throw the tantrums, and, besides — it brings the wrinkles. *Oh, la, la*, please go and do something about your face. I will get us some lunch — if it is possible to prepare it in this primitive hovel.'

She threw off her sweater, turned back her shirt sleeves, and tied a towel round her waist. As Francesca applied cold compresses to her swollen eyes,

Gabrielle whisked eggs, herbs, and touches of anything else on hand, into an omelette that was a miracle of lightness.

As the two women ate their lunch they talked easily, but Gabrielle did not pry into Francesca's plans and, despite their new truce — even friendship — Francesca could not bring herself to mention Adam's suspicions of her nefarious activities at Lynford. She thanked Gabrielle warmly for her offers of help in finding work in Paris, but would only say, as Gabrielle drove off, waving and still marvelling at her self-imposed exile, that she would consider her next move and let Gabrielle know before she left France for good.

7

After Gabrielle had gone, Francesca
returned to the cottage. She managed
to wash up their lunch dishes with
shaking hands, then she huddled into
the old velvet armchair by the window.
She felt shattered by Gabrielle's revelations, completely unable to organise her
feelings to accommodate the new
situation. Her knowledge that Adam
had behaved honourably in this matter,
too, did little to relieve her despair over
her own love for him, convinced as she
was that he still loved Gabrielle whatever
ulterior purpose she had used him for.

And how cruel Gabrielle's use of him
had been in the circumstances — a passionate man, deeply in love, in constant
attendance, yet unable to touch her. No
wonder that, in his frustration, he had
been tempted to make love to Francesca.
She knew herself, all too well now, the

fierceness of the body's demands.

His cynical views on love and marriage were understandable, when his mistress of many years had left him for his wealthy friend — a repetition, apparently, of his mother's behaviour years earlier. And it explained his conviction that Francesca, too, had been on the look-out all along for a generous protector.

Well, there was nothing she could do about his hang-ups in that area, but his mistaken conviction that she had been involved, with Drew, in the criminal activities at Lynford increasingly rankled. It was totally unfair, and the fact that she had been unjustly and self-righteously reproaching him all the time he was convinced of her involvement in the sickening business was particularly upsetting to her. How he must have despised her.

She resolved to make a last effort to clear her name — simply to leave would be an admission of guilt — and the only possibility seemed to lie with Drew. Adam refused to believe a word she said to him, but, if she could only persuade Drew to clear her, maybe Adam would listen to him.

It was good to have come to some sort of decision, but it was too late today to put it into practice. She didn't want to ask Sylvie for transport; she had memorised the bus timetable outside the village bar and a bus left at noon every day for Paris. She would leave the following day, post the cottage keys back to Sylvie with her thanks, make an attempt to get Drew to clear her in Adam's eyes, then quit Paris for good.

She got to her feet and began to tidy the cottage, then packed most of her belongings ready for departure. It seemed a very long evening, although she went to bed early as there was nothing left to do.

The following morning she woke very early after a miserable and disturbed night, and realised that she was not going to get back to sleep again.

It was a beautiful day. The early morning sun crept through the sweet-scented roses massed against her window and the birdsong was poignantly sweet. Francesca lay for a minute, tears forming in her eyes and a lump in her throat. It seemed to her that the very summit of heaven would be for Adam to be beside her now, his lips on her hair and mouth, his hands caressing her.

She shuddered and jumped out of bed. She must not allow her mind to stray along such lines, in a way that reduced her to longing helplessness. Certainly not when she might have to face him for a last time.

She bathed, dressed, finished her packing and forced herself to eat some breakfast. It was still barely ten o'clock. Even burdened with luggage, it shouldn't take her more than forty minutes to walk to St. Clément. She decided to fill the time with a last walk up the hill to the trees to fill her lungs with the sweet country air before she returned to the city.

★   ★   ★

She closed and bolted all the shutters and, locking the front door behind her, set off up the overgrown drive. The sun was already warm as she left the road and crossed the short-cropped grass to the knoll of trees, but, once beneath the trees, as before, she was in a cool, quiet world. The only sound was that of a car engine seemingly closer than usual. She froze, straining her ears to listen. At the very moment that the engine stopped, she realised that the sound had come from behind her, from the direction of the cottage.

She spun round and began to retrace her footsteps swiftly, then at a stumbling run, scarcely daring to breathe. She could see the gold lasers of sunlight ahead through the trees, when a gnarled root caught her foot and she pitched headlong to the ground. She started to scramble to her feet, when the pain in one ankle caused her to subside again, gritting her teeth in pain. The ankle that she had damaged in her fall in the Bois de Boulogne, still weakened, had collapsed again.

She clutched at a convenient branch and managed to pull herself upright. Then, grimacing with pain, she began to make her way to the end of the path, supporting herself from branch to tree trunk along the way. Her progress seemed interminable, but at last she reached the edge of the trees and her eyes flew anxiously towards the cottage. Adam's Renault stood outside.

There was no sign of Adam. Instinctively Francesca released her hold to start down the long sweep of grass that separated them, only to collapse on to her hands and knees. As she crouched helplessly, wincing at the hot jab of pain from her foot, Adam appeared from around the back of the house. He looked up at the shuttered windows and, with a stab of despair, she realised how unoccupied the house must look. As he shook the locked front door, she cursed her care in securing the house behind her.

She rose upright on her knees and called his name, but he showed no sign of having heard. Sudden fear washed over her. Apart from the frustration of not being able to reach Adam, she would not be able to reach the cottage or the road, let alone St. Clément. She would be stranded here alone and helpless on the edge of this dark wood, and eventually night would fall . . .

She reared up again and called his name at the top pitch of her lungs, but still he did not look in her direction. Oh, God, let him look this way, she prayed. He would immediately spot her yellow dress against the dark trees. Desperately she crawled the few feet back to the wood and, hanging on to a bough, hauled herself upright.

Adam had returned to the car now; his hand was on the door. With tears of love almost blinding her, Francesca noted the indolent grace of his body as he turned back again. He put up a hand to shade his eyes from the sun and looked up the hill. His gaze seemed to range in an arc almost to her, then he turned once again to the car. Summoning all her strength, Francesca screamed his name.

He stopped, as though frozen, and turned round quickly. His eyes were searching the horizon now. Francesca yelled again and waved, clutching the tree as she almost collapsed.

He had seen her. He gave a half-wave and started easily up the hill, not perceiving any drama in the situation then, after a few yards, perhaps wondering why she did not advance to meet him but continued clinging to a tree, he hastened his steps. Already, from this distance, Francesca could see a frown knitting his dark brows. It looked as though she had succeeded in annoying him once again.

She let herself slide down to the grass and sat awaiting him, an apologetic expression on her face, until he reached her and was standing over her, glaring down at her with a mixture of worry and irritation.

'What the hell have you done now?' he demanded.

It was not exactly the lovers' meeting she had dreamed of. Francesca fought back her tears. 'It isn't anything new, it's the same thing,' she attempted to explain. 'I mean, it's the ankle I hurt in the Bois de Boulogne. It's gone again.'

'And didn't it occur to you that it might not be up to cross-country hikes?'

'I wasn't on a cross-country hike. I was just going for a short walk, when I heard the car behind me and I — I ran back,' her voice tailed off.

★ ★ ★

Adam knelt beside her. He removed her sandal and manipulated her ankle in his strong hands. Francesca gasped and bit back a moan. He looked at her white face.

'Didn't that hurt?'

'Yes.'

'Then why didn't you say?'

'I was trying not to make a fuss.'

'My dear girl, the whole point of the operation is to find out where it hurts.

Stop trying to be a heroine.' He moved the foot again and she yelped obligingly.

'You don't have to deafen me. What on earth was the idea of this ridiculous retreat, anyway? This — this living off nuts and berries?'

'I wasn't doing anything of the sort. It was a holiday. A break from the city.' Francesca looked down at his smooth dark head in which the sun had found reddish lights. She fought an almost overwhelming urge to stroke it. 'Why did you come after me?' she ventured, in a small voice. 'You aren't responsible for me. I'm not in your employ now.'

'I came looking for you because there was no living with Nicole, or Celestine — or Vachette either,' he muttered without looking at her. 'They haven't uttered a civil word to me since you left. And someone has to be responsible for you, you seem remarkably accident prone.'

'I never used to be,' she countered indignantly. 'It's only since I came to Paris.'

He smiled. 'I've heard Paris held responsible for a lot of things, but never spraining ankles at a distance of thirty kilometres.'

'I just meant that — somehow I used to be much more self-reliant.'

'I know what you mean.' His voice was gentler, but his face was a blank mask. 'And it has nothing to do with Paris.'

He slipped her sandal back on and stood up. 'Well, it's obvious you won't be walking very far for a few days. Stay there!' he ordered, as he turned away.

'Where are you going?' Francesca wailed.

He looked back at her. 'I have no intention of carrying you two hundred yards with a perfectly good car at my disposal.'

Watching his retreating back striding down the hill, Francesca realised that their relationship was going to be just as prickly and defensive as it had from the start. She leant her head against the tree trunk, feeling faint and slightly sick.

In a few minutes the car pulled up

at the edge of the wood and Adam jumped out, real concern on his face. He knelt beside her once again. 'Are you OK?'

Francesca nodded wanly.

'Hang on there, sweetheart.' He gathered her up in his arms, and, for a second, her head rested against his strong shoulder, then he eased her into the passenger seat and they drove slowly and bumpily over the grass.

Outside the cottage, he took the key from her and went inside, opening doors and shutters, then he returned and, lifting her easily from the car, carried her inside.

He carried her to the bedroom and put her down gently on the bed. As he left the room, Francesca lay back, her eyes closed, feeling quite unable to deal with this new situation. She had been geared up to one last meeting with Adam, in an attempt to clear her name. She had planned to be quite unemotional, not reproachful, but magnanimous in forgiveness, should she succeed. Now,

264

here she was again, a stupid, weak, defence-less victim dependent on his whims.

'Is there anything to drink in this place?' his voice came from the kitchen.

'No, I finished the wine.'

He grunted. She heard him leave the house, and the car door open and shut. A moment later he appeared with a silver hip flask.

'I carry this in case I should get caught in mountain snowdrifts. Or meet with damsels in distress.' He poured a measure into the cap and handed it to her before leaving the room again.

*   *   *

Almost immediately, as she sipped the brandy, a relaxing warmth began to steal over her. When Adam returned, carrying a bowl of water and towels, she was sitting up, a faint pink glow in her cheeks. He had taken off his jacket and turned back the cuffs of his shirt.

He looked at her approvingly. 'Good. You're looking a bit brighter.' He put a thickly wadded towel on the bed and wrung a linen cloth out in the water. Then he lifted Francesca's bare brown leg and wrapped the cloth tightly around her ankle.

She gasped at the icy shock of the cloth, but almost at once there was some relief from the nagging ache in the joint.

'Better?' Adam asked.

'Much better.' Francesca leaned back against the pillows again. She forced herself to look straight at him and meet his eyes, something she had been avoiding since the start of their encounter. 'Thank you. I'm sorry I've been so much trouble.'

To her amazement, Adam's face flushed a deep scarlet. He concentrated on screwing the cap back on his flask. 'You've certainly been trouble,' he agreed. 'More than you'll ever know.'

The fragile confidence that the brandy had given her shattered instantly at his blunt words, and bright tears sprang to her eyes.

She forced herself to ask again, 'Then

why did you come after me? I didn't want you to.' The words emerged rough with unshed tears.

'You know perfectly well why I had to find you.' His eyes still avoided hers. 'I misjudged you cruelly and if you can't bring yourself to forgive me — I'll quite understand.'

There was a moment's silence. Francesca whispered, 'Forgive you?'

He took both her hands in his, and now he looked at her. 'For believing you were involved in the destruction of the Lynford books and had cheated, and made a fool of, my uncle. Oh, Francesca, how could I? Nicole, Vachette, Sylvie, Celestine — they all believed in your integrity. Only I couldn't trust you. You were simply too good to be true.'

A tremulous smile broke through on Francesca's face, although her eyes were still starry with tears. 'Thank goodness, you believe me at last. I couldn't bear to leave France knowing you still thought such terrible things about me.'

His grip tightened on her hands and his eyes pleaded with her, his arrogant pride humbled. 'Please say you forgive me! I treated you so vilely.'

'Oh, Adam, of course I forgive you. If what you thought had been true, no treatment of me could have been bad enough. And you had convincing reasons. What made you finally believe me?'

He released her hands abruptly, rose and looked out of the window. 'Drew,' he said shortly.

'Drew cleared me?' Francesca was surprised that it had been so easy. 'I was going to see him, to plead with him to intercede with you.'

'You probably wouldn't have been successful.'

'But he told you.'

'After I beat it out of him.'

'*What?*' Francesca stared at him. It was impossible to connect such a primitive action with the cool, sophisticated, expensively-clad man outlined against the window.

'I had to beat it out of him.' He

returned to the bed and stood awkwardly at the foot, gripping the old-
fashioned bed-end. For the first time,
Francesca noticed that the knuckles of
his left hand were freshly grazed.

'I went to see him in his room. I — I
just couldn't bear not knowing the truth.
He laughed at me — he wasn't exactly
sober — and I knocked him down. That
sobered him up in a hurry. He said he
had thought of using you when he first
saw you in such a trusted position at the
shop, but he realised right away that you
were so straight and honest it was a
non-starter. Anyone could see that, he
said. Anyone,' Adam repeated bitterly.
'Even Drew. Everybody except me.'

★   ★   ★

Francesca made a small embarrassed
gesture with her hands. Adam sat down
on the bed beside her and gathered
them in his own again.

'And then, just at that point, a girl
came into the room and the last piece

269

slotted into place. Because she could have been described in exactly the same terms as you — dark blonde hair, brown eyes, a good figure — although there was no real resemblance. This was Drew's accomplice.

'I walked out and left them, but I've written to Drew since. I told him I'm not pressing charges and I've offered to buy the atlases from him — at a favourable price to myself.' He smiled wryly. 'I must preserve my reputation as a hard businessman.'

'Poor Drew,' Francesca said softly, thinking of the bright, high-spirited boy who had once meant so much to her.

'You did love him, didn't you?' Adam asked gently.

'I suppose I did — in a way. It was a long time ago and part of growing up.'

'I'm sorry it had to turn out like this.'

'You couldn't help it, and it's all over now.'

All over now, she repeated to herself. She could return to England with her reputation restored and take up her old life again and perhaps, in time, this whole Paris interlude would be just a memory.

Suddenly, Adam's presence in the small room, on the bed beside her, just as he had been in her dreams, was more than she could bear. Helpless tears gathered in her eyes, but Adam was engrossed in renewing her bandage.

'You haven't told me how you came to find me,' she said thickly.

'Gabrielle told me you were here. She telephoned last night and suggested it might be a good idea for me to talk to you.' He dried his hands. 'I'd just cleared matters up with Drew and I was desperate to find you and put things right between us.'

'Gabrielle told me the truth about your relationship with her.' Francesca struggled on, 'I didn't know that she and Gaston had only recently been married, or that he had only recently been crippled, and that your affair was over by then. Drew, probably deliberately, never mentioned it, and I suppose

271

Sylvie assumed I knew. I misjudged you, too, Adam. Not only over your treatment of Mr. Pinkerton, but about your affair with Gabrielle as well.'

'It was stupid,' Adam burst out. 'A stupid charade. It suited us well enough while there was no one else, but it was cruel to Gaston — even though he had suggested it out of love for Gabrielle.'

'And to you?' The words nearly choked her, but she had to know the answer. 'Was it painful for you?'

He looked at her, genuinely surprised.

'I mean,' she pressed on, 'were you still in love with Gabrielle when she left you for Gaston?'

'No. It had been good — I don't want to knock it — but it had gone stale. I suppose it was a bit of a blow to my pride — just one more example of woman's fickleness — but, really, it had been over for a long time. And you made me realise what an immoral set-up it was.'

'Just my small-town morals.' She attempted a smile. 'It was nothing to do with me. I was only your employee.'

'You were never only that.' The tension in Adam's body, in the whole room, was palpable now. He rose and paced to the window, his back towards her. 'And it was, I hoped, a lot to do with you.'

His voice was so low that Francesca thought she had misheard him. 'Why?' she ventured.

There was a brief pause. Then Adam said, 'Because I loved you.'

'What?' Francesca asked stupidly.

'I loved you.' He spun round. 'Do I have to spell it out for you?' he demanded almost angrily. 'I loved you from the first moment I saw you at the station with your heart-stopping beauty. And I loved you more every day that I knew you — your sweetness and loyalty, your spirit and fun and intelligence. And festering all the time at the back of my addled brain was the conviction that the whole thing was an act, the very clever act that had ensnared my uncle and Drew, and I was going to make damned sure it didn't work on me!'

★ ★ ★

There was a long silence. Adam glared at her, his violet eyes hard with unshed tears, as though defying her to humble him further.

'Oh, Adam, I love you so.' Francesca held out her arms. 'You must come to me, my love, I can't come to you.'

He was beside her in an instant. He gathered her into his arms and kissed her as though he could never be sated — her mouth, her eyes, her throat. For the first few minutes there was nothing but simple joy between them, at the resolving of misunderstanding and the admission of love. Then Francesca felt that new emotion take possession of her.

Her blood began to pulse through her veins with a throbbing insistent beat, and her skin craved for his touch. He responded instantly to her change of mood. His hands moved over her and his kisses grew more urgent and demanding. His dark head bent down and his lips touched her neck with featherlight kisses until she could have screamed for him to stop, or go further.

His own control began to slip. His hand moved down to caress the curve of her waist, her hip. His breath came harshly, his body grew tense and a moan broke from him. She would have gone with him, sinking deeper and deeper into ecstasy, if he hadn't suddenly broken away from her and lain on his back, his breath ragged and uneven.

As his body left hers, Francesca felt a pain of deprivation that was almost physical. She clung to him, twining her arms around his neck.

Adam seized her two wrists and held her away from him. 'No, Francesca! You're driving me too far. The last thing I want is another mistress.'

Shocked, she backed away from him. 'You don't want me? You were putting on a very convincing performance a moment ago!'

The emotions of the past hour finally

took their toll and tears started to rain down her face. She attempted to flee from the bed, but her damaged ankle buckled under her, and Adam grabbed her from behind to stop her falling. He held her tightly round the waist and buried his hot face in the nape of her neck.

'Oh, darling! Want you? I'm nearly out of my mind with wanting you. It's just that I don't want to find myself back in the same old unsatisfying situation — not one thing or another. Gabrielle was safe, familiar. She didn't make deep emotional demands — plenty of material ones, maybe, but not of feelings. And that suited me. I suppose a psychiatrist could have told me that there were reasons in my past why I was afraid of totally giving myself. Then — a little over two years ago, I began to realise what love could really be.'

'Two years ago.' She could not keep the dismay out of her voice and was glad that he could not see her face.

She forced out the words. 'You met someone else?'

'Not met. But letters began to arrive from my uncle, letters all about a girl who had come to work for him. And, as he described her, I began to see what it would be like to let go, to completely love another human being — the pain as well as the joy. I wasn't quite ready to take a chance, but Gabrielle wasn't enough any more.'

She squirmed round in his arms to face him, a tremulous smile on her bruised mouth. 'Adam, I only want to be with you.'

'But I want you for my wife and nothing less.' He began to laugh shakily. 'Uncle Oswald was a very good letter-writer, very persuasive. Then he sent me that photograph that I looked at until I nearly wore it out. You know, darling — I wouldn't be surprised if this was exactly what the old rascal had in mind all along!'

They kissed gently as he cradled her in his arms. The sun passed through its meridian and the shadows lengthened in the room as they made their plans and promises, and Francesca knew finally that her wayward heart had not led her astray, but had chosen right and true.

THE END

We do hope that you have enjoyed reading this large print book.

Did you know that all of our titles are available for purchase?

We publish a wide range of high quality large print books including:
Romances, Mysteries, Classics
General Fiction
Non Fiction and Westerns

Special interest titles available in large print are:
The Little Oxford Dictionary
Music Book, Song Book
Hymn Book, Service Book

Also available from us courtesy of Oxford University Press:
Young Readers' Dictionary
(large print edition)
Young Readers' Thesaurus
(large print edition)

For further information or a free brochure, please contact us at:
Ulverscroft Large Print Books Ltd.,
The Green, Bradgate Road, Anstey,
Leicester, LE7 7FU, England.
Tel: (00 44) **0116 236 4325**
Fax: (00 44) **0116 234 0205**

Lorna had come to Cyprus reluctantly, as her aunt's holiday companion. There she met James, who helped her to find out that there was more to the island than hotels and beaches. But could he save her when a ruthless scheme to exploit the island's beauty put her in deadly danger? What would happen to their growing friendship when the holiday was over? And what were her aunt's secret plans?

CHATEAU OF THE NYMPH

Sheila Daglish

When Jenna goes to work in her aunt's French hotel, she finds that someone is determined to force her family out. Is it the darkly forbidding Luc de Villiers? Centuries ago, the son of the lord of the chateau had fallen in love with the girl from the village inn. Was history repeating itself? Only when Jenna's life is put in danger does she discover the truth behind the chateau's legend and find love in place of long-ago tragedy.

LORD ATHERTON'S WARD

Fenella Miller

When their father, Sir John, dies leaving Sarah Ellison and her younger sister Jane orphaned, his choice of guardian is entirely disagreeable to Sarah — particularly with Lord Atherton's insistence that they leave their family home and move to Highfield Hall to remain under the care of his mother. The young, passionate Sarah refuses to bow down to the command of anyone — but will her headstrong behaviour alienate Lord Atherton, or prove that she is a girl he can respect?